She dared not give, not take

"No!" Andrea cried aloud and tore herself from his arms. "I won't! I can't!"

Startled, Luke stared at her. "Why not? You want me as much as I want you."

"Don't read more into it than was there." The effort of hiding her feelings robbed her voice of color, and it came out flat and cold. "You're an attractive devil and you caught me at a vulnerable moment."

"I had the impression it was more than that."

"It wasn't," she said indifferently.

"Pity. We'd be good together."

ROBERTA LEIGH wrote her first book at the age of nineteen and since then has written more than seventy romance novels, as well as many books and film series for children. She has also been an editor of a woman's magazine and produced a teen magazine, but writing romance fiction remains one of her greatest joys. She lives in Hampstead, London, and has one son.

Books by Roberta Leigh

ROBERTA LEIGH

BACHELOR AT HEART

Harlequin Books

TORONTO • NEW YORK • LONDON
AMSTERDAM • PARIS • SYDNEY • HAMBURG
STOCKHOLM • ATHENS • TOKYO • MILAN
MADRID • WARSAW • BUDAPEST • AUCKLAND

Harlequin Presents Plus first edition July 1993
ISBN 0-373-11568-7

Original hardcover edition published in 1992
by Mills & Boon Limited

BACHELOR AT HEART

CHAPTER ONE

'THERE'S no way I'll ever agree to work for Luke Kane,' Andrea Markham stated firmly. 'We had a terrible row and I don't want anything to do with him.'

Bella Jessel, widow of the man who, until his death a week ago, had successfully guided Andrea's career, stared at her in astonishment. 'I had no idea you knew him. When did you quarrel?'

'Twelve years ago—when he was still working for your agency.'

'But you were only a child then!'

'A thirteen-year-old is still capable of feelings.'

'Of course,' Bella acknowledged. 'But not of judgement. I'd be surprised if Luke even remembered you'd quarrelled.'

'That's beside the point,' Andrea replied. '*I* remember; and I'm sure he hasn't changed. If anything, success has probably made him *more* insufferable.'

'Abraham didn't find him so or he wouldn't have sold him the agency.' Bella's eyes filled with tears as she spoke of her husband. 'I take it he didn't know how you felt about Luke?'

'No. There was never any reason to mention it.' Andrea hesitated, then fell silent, reluctant to explain further.

Momentarily Bella closed her eyes, revealing the darkness of sleepless nights on her lids. 'Abraham wasn't going to tell you he'd sold his agency until after your tour was over, because he didn't wish you to know how ill he was. But he was so happy that you'd finally overcome your phobia about playing in front of a live audience.'

'I can't do it without him,' Andrea cried huskily. 'I can't!'

'You must. He wanted it so much for you. He was proud of his artists, but *you* had a special place in his heart.'

Andrea's thoughts winged back to the gauche seventeen-year-old who had managed to summon up the courage to approach the great man. He had agreed to see her because she had told his secretary she was the stepsister of Gillian Brown, who had worked for him three years earlier and had once been engaged to Luke Kane, his young assistant at that time.

'I'd like you to hear me play,' she had stated when face to face with him. 'I've a lot to learn yet, but I'll work like a demon to get to the top.'

Unsmiling, Abraham Jessel had indicated the Bechstein grand in the corner of the room. She had played two Chopin pieces and a Brahms, and when she finished he had regarded her silently, then announced he would talk to her stepmother regarding further tuition.

For the next four years she had not seen him, and not until she had graduated from the Juilliard School of Music in New York and returned to London had he come to see her and offered to be her agent. She had agreed instantly, and only then had her stepmother informed her it was Abraham who had paid her tuition fees, insisting the money was a gift and not to be repaid.

'Thank goodness I signed with him,' Andrea had exclaimed. 'I'd have felt terrible if I'd gone to someone else.'

'If you had, he wouldn't have allowed me to tell you. He's that sort of man. You're a lucky girl to have him manage your career.'

It was a luck Andrea appreciated. Within a few months she was booked for recording sessions in England and abroad. Not only did Abraham seek out the best contracts for her, but he also transformed her from gauche girl to sophisticated woman.

He persuaded her to drop the childish 'Annie', and assume her proper name of Andrea, as well as taking her mother's maiden name, which was more impressive than Jones. He also sent her on a month's modelling course, from which an entirely different creature emerged. Her long, unruly black hair had been tamed into a gleaming black satin pageboy. Parted in the middle, it fell either side of her face and framed translucent pearly skin. Straggly dark eyebrows had been shaped into delicate arcs that complemented almond-shaped eyes, whose colour resembled the heart of a pansy—darkest indigo blue with a hint of violet. A small mouth with a full lower lip, slightly tip-tilted nose and rounded yet determined chin had no need for change, while her naturally slender figure presented no problems to the famous couturier into whose hands Abraham had entrusted her.

This last modification—from chain-store conformity to individual chic—was the final act in her metamorphosis. Yet the new-found elegance and confidence were only on the outside: a façade hiding her burning determination to succeed, to prove to the world—and one particular man in it—that she was a person to be respected, and not a shadow of her stepsister.

As fame and success enveloped her and she stood in her own spotlight, proving her worth to this man became unimportant, and he faded from her mind. Indeed, until today she had believed she had forgotten him. Which went to show what tricks the mind could play!

'My dear, please do the concerts.' Bella's words brought Andrea back to the present. 'I realise it won't be the same without Abraham, but I'm sure Luke will do all he can to see everything goes smoothly. Talk to him at least.'

Andrea was hard put to it not to refuse, yet for Abraham's sake she couldn't. 'Very well, I'll go see him. But I'm not promising anything more.'

Later that day she asked her secretary to fix the appointment. Luke was out of town and the earliest he could see her was the end of the week. It gave her four long days to mull over the best way of dealing with the situation, and she still hadn't reached a conclusion when Friday dawned. Deciding to play it by ear, since it depended to a large extent on how difficult Luke Kane would be over relinquishing her contract, she concentrated instead on what to wear. Was it better to look assured and sophisticated, casual and nonchalant, or gentle and seductive? But what the hell! Why should she care *what* impression she gave? If Luke wouldn't release her she'd fight for her freedom.

In the event, she settled on being herself, choosing an amethyst silk shirt-waister that emphasised the violet of her eyes, and twisting her hair into its usual chignon. Because she was pale, always a sign that she was nervous, she was slightly heavier with her make-up, though she appeared the epitome of confidence as she entered the luxuriously appointed offices of Kane Enterprises, in an elegant white stone building off Grosvenor Square; a contrast indeed from the old-fashioned suite of rooms where Abraham had conducted his business, which Luke had left the same year her stepsister had left *him*.

As she walked through the thickly carpeted reception area she glanced at the photographs of the famous musicians lining the walls. Abraham's clients had not yet been added, but even without them, Luke's list was impressive.

'Mr Kane will see you right away,' the young receptionist said, leading her along a wide corridor to a heavy black quilted leather door at the end. Pushing it open, she stepped aside to let Andrea enter.

Her first impression was of a large room where luxury and the highly functional went hand in hand: an enormous glass and steel table was stacked with files, a battery of telephones and a fax machine, which momentarily struck her as affectation until she realised they were essential for keeping in touch with artists throughout the world. The wall on her left housed the latest stereo and television systems, and the one on her right shelves of records, cassettes and video recordings.

Steeling herself, she met Luke's eyes as he walked across the room to greet her, hand outstretched.

'Miss Markham,' he smiled. 'It's a pleasure to meet you, though I'm sorry it isn't in happier circumstances.'

'In happier circumstances we wouldn't have met,' Andrea replied coolly, and saw his dark eyebrows draw together, though he made no comment as he motioned her to an armchair.

What was he thinking? she wondered, looking at him candidly. He had changed little in the twelve years since she had seen him, maturing from a tensely dynamic and voluble young man into a tensely dynamic, restrained thirty-six-year-old, with a lithe body, a tanned, unlined face, and jet-black hair. His chiselled features showed no sign of age: moulded cheekbones, straight nose, wide, well-shaped mouth and firm chin with no hint of slackness. His eccentricity hadn't changed either, she noted, aware of the designer stubble on the square jaw, and his thick, glossy hair, drawn back into a neat ponytail that complemented his casual yet expensive clothes. True, the jeans and sweat-shirt were now replaced by a blue cashmere sweater and navy Ralph Lauren trousers, but he still did not wear a suit, as Abraham had constantly urged him to do, and looked more like a promoter of rock concerts than classical ones.

But had he listened to Abraham it would have been out of character, for though his clientele consisted of classical musicians, he presented them to the public with the hype and glamour normally associated with rock artists. This had attracted audiences who would never ordinarily have listened to them, and his *Catchy Classics* and *Best Loved Arias* had proved to be extraordinarily popular and financially successful.

Andrea waited for him to make some comment on herself, but he merely settled himself in a chair opposite her and crossed one long leg over the other.

'Your photographs don't do you justice, Miss Markham.' Grey eyes slowly appraised her. 'But photographs rarely do—any more than recordings.'

'Do you really think so? About recordings, I mean?' she asked, surprised.

'Definitely. We may have reached technical perfection, but we can't totally capture the essence of a personality on film or tape. And a good thing too, or I'd be out of business!'

'Instead of which you make a fortune,' she stated.

'But I don't intend you to make one from me.'

'Ah!' he said slowly. 'So that's why you're here.'

'Yes.'

He leaned forward and she couldn't help noticing how silky his hair was. She had an almost irresistible urge to touch it, and she caught her breath. Was she experiencing a resurgence of her teenage crush? Humiliated by the notion, she sat up straighter. 'I don't want you to be my agent,' she said.

'Why not?'

There was an incisive edge to his smooth tone that she did not like. What game was he playing? 'You know very well why not,' she replied icily.

A phone on his desk rang, and with a murmured apology he rose to answer it. There followed a spate of voluble Italian before the call ended and he returned to his chair.

'Sorry about that,' he said, 'but to continue... I've no idea what you have against me, Miss Markham. I can only assume you feel such intense loyalty to Abraham Jessel that you're unhappy to be represented by the man who was his biggest rival. But you've no need to be. He *wanted* me to buy his business. In fact, *he* approached *me*.'

'I know. Bella—Mrs Jessel—told me. But it doesn't alter the way I feel. I don't want you representing me.'

'I'd like to know why,' he repeated. 'Granted, I promote my artists differently from the way Abraham did, but——'

'It's got nothing to do with that!'

'What, then?' His voice was bland. 'If I've offended you in any way, I'm quite unaware of it.'

'Don't give me that!' she exploded.

'Are you trying to tell me we've met before?' Silvergrey eyes met hers in genuine surprise; incredibly, he hadn't recognised her.

'The last time we saw each other,' she said, 'my name was Annie.'

He stared at her, and she saw his expression change from confusion to astonishment. 'Good lord! Gillian's kid sister.' He grinned broadly, suddenly the boyish Luke she had once known. 'You should be pleased I didn't recognise you. You were a skinny, gawky kid with frizzy hair and braces on your teeth!'

'Thanks!' she said scathingly. 'I see your manners haven't improved!'

He went on staring at her. 'So *you're* Annie,' he murmured, ignoring her remark. 'But what did I do to annoy you? From what I remember, we were always friends.'

Realising he had no recollection of the hurt he had inflicted on her served to increase Andrea's anger. 'I thought we were friends too, until you almost threw me out of your office when I last saw you.'

His expression went blank, the light seeping from his eyes as he retreated to the past. Watching him, she was sorry she had raised it. Airing old grievances rarely did any good, and in this case had only served to show Luke she was still hurt by something *he* didn't even remember! How amused he would be to know she had deeply missed the monthly concerts to which he had taken her, and that her schoolgirl crush on him had taken years to fade.

'It's coming back to me now,' he muttered, and looked at her again with seeing eyes. 'You came to tell me Gillian had gone off with someone else, and I was so bitter that I let it out on *you*.'

'Bitter!' Andrea jeered. 'That's a laugh! You ran around with every woman in sight, yet were furious when Gillian left you flat.'

'That isn't my interpretation of events,' came the dry response. 'But it's a lifetime ago and we should be thinking of today. You need me, and——'

'You aren't the only impresario!'

'I'm one of the best.'

'I don't care. I prefer to go to someone else.'

'You aren't free to do so.' He rose and paced the carpet: a tall, slim figure, vibrant with energy. 'I've taken over Abraham's artists, and you—under my management—can be a valuable property. One I don't wish to lose.'

'I'm willing to buy my contract from you. I'll ask my lawyer to——'

'Money doesn't enter into it,' Luke cut in. 'I'd envy *anyone* who represented you. You are the finest pianist I've heard and I don't think you've reached your peak yet.'

'I'm overwhelmed,' she scoffed.

'I'm the one who's overwhelmed,' he said softly. 'I can't believe little Annie Jones is the famous Andrea Markham. I must have been blind not to have recognised you from your pictures!' His eyes, disturbingly intent, ranged over her, and his lips curved in a smile, showing their sensuality. 'I still think of you as Annie, but I'll do my best to call you Andrea.'

Try though she did to resist him, Andrea found him more devastating today than years ago. Or was it because today she was a woman and not a schoolgirl? A woman, and therefore more vulnerable. It was an alarming thought.

'Don't worry about the tour,' he said unexpectedly, his words indicating that he had noticed the fright on her face, though thankfully he had misinterpreted the reason. 'I'll look after you as well as Abraham would have done.'

'I want to cancel it,' she stated, knowing that now, more than ever, she could not face it. 'I should never have agreed to it.'

'None the less, you *did*. If you call it off, Abraham's estate will suffer.'

'What do you mean?'

'Everything has been booked and paid for: halls, orchestras, conductors, flights, hotels.'

Andrea jumped to her feet. 'What if I'd been taken ill and genuinely couldn't perform?'

'Abraham was insured against that possibility,' Luke replied. 'But there's no insurance against the tantrums of a hysterical artist.'

'Hysterical?' She flinched. No, she was damned if she'd admit it was her fear of crowds, not temperament, that made a live audience so terrifying to her. Trying to hide her trembling, she sat down again. 'I've only given one public concert,' she said stiffly, 'and it was a disaster.'

'That was years ago. You've matured since,' he argued.

'I still can't do it.'

'Every artist has stage fright, Andrea. But I'll be with you and I promise everything will be fine.'

'I tell you, I don't *want* to go on the tour and I don't want *you* to represent me!' she cried exasperatedly. 'Won't seeing me remind you of Gillian? For that reason alone I thought you'd be happy to release me from my contract.'

'Gillian's on the other side of the world, and I can live with the fact that you're her sister.' Luke leaned against the side of the glass-topped table, arms folded across his chest, long legs relaxed. 'So the answer is no. I won't release you.'

Her temper rose. Luke was as arrogant and dogmatic as ever. 'You can't force me to stay with you. If necessary, I'll give up music and retire!'

He laughed. 'Music is your life.'

'Don't bet on it,' she snapped.

He went to speak, thought better of it, and silently sauntered round the side of the table to sit in the black leather swing chair, his tanned skin and jet-black hair completing a picture of saturnine magnificence. So must the devil look, Andrea thought with a shiver.

'It will cost you a bomb to fight me,' he said quietly. 'Though as you've made a fortune, I don't suppose the money will worry you. But spare a thought for Bella. She could be broke at the end of it all.'

'Why? If this is some trick of yours...'

'It's no trick. Abraham's agency has already paid the expenses of your tour, and if you cancel it they'll suffer a terrific loss. It's an open secret he lost a fortune on the stock exchange six months ago, and he was counting on your tour to bail him out of trouble. Even if you don't give a hang for Bella, you should do it out of loyalty to

Abraham. He loved her and would be devastated if she was left virtually penniless.'

Andrea was appalled. Was Luke lying about her late manager's finances to force her hand?

'I'm not lying,' Luke said as if he were telepathic. 'You can talk to Abraham's executor.'

Andrea shook her head, knowing when she was beaten. 'I—I'll do the concerts if you promise to release me at the end of them.'

'Sure.'

His instant acquiescence alerted her. 'Put it in writing and send it to my lawyer.'

'Don't you trust me?' There was amusement in his tone.

'No.' There was none in hers.

'I'll see he has it first thing tomorrow.'

'Thank you.'

'Of course, there's one thing you haven't considered,' he added.

'Which is?'

'When the tour's over you may elect to stay with me!'

'Pigs might fly!' she retorted, and walked smartly to the door.

'Annie!'

She spun round.

'Just checking to see if you still responded to your real name,' he grinned.

With a supreme effort she held on to her temper and quietly closed the door on him. What had she let herself in for? she wondered soberly as she left the building. Coping with a live audience was going to be nerve-racking enough, but coping with Luke Kane looked as if it might be even worse.

CHAPTER TWO

CAUGHT in a traffic jam on the way home, Andrea had ample opportunity to reflect on the past and Luke, and to admit that though he had caused her a great deal of pain as a teenager, his casual disregard for her burgeoning musical ability had had the paradoxical effect of goading her into making music her career.

She had once mentioned this in passing to Abraham, who had defended him by saying that even the best impresario could make mistakes.

Andrea had sniffed. 'After all the training you gave him, I think it was disloyal of him to leave you and start up on his own.'

'I did the same when I was his age,' Abraham had smiled. 'It's natural for fledgelings to want to fly the nest.'

'The most talented musicians still come to you,' she had commented triumphantly.

'One day they'll go to Luke. And he will serve them well.'

She thought of this now and, inevitably, it led her to her stepsister. Did Gillian ever regret not telling him to his face that she was going to marry another man, or did she still think she had been right to simply walk out on him?

'You can't go without a word!' Andrea had protested when Gillian had informed her she intended marrying Peter Maynard, a young Australian she had met three months earlier.

'Why not?' her stepsister had retorted. 'If Luke can date other women when he's supposed to be in love with me, he doesn't deserve any better.'

'You told me they were his clients!'

'Because I didn't want to disillusion you. But it's time you grew up and saw him for what he is—a two-timing womaniser!'

'He always seems so devoted to you,' Andrea had argued.

'You're too young to see through his act,' Gillian had said bitterly. 'But since he started up on his own I've hardly seen him.'

'If you loved him you'd put up with it.'

'Must you always defend him?' Gillian had cried. 'I think he cares more about *you* than me, the way he's always taking you out!'

'Only to concerts—which he knows you hate,' Andrea had said, thinking how silly Gillian could be. 'Anyway, if he were having affairs with other women he wouldn't *want* me to go with him!'

'You're his alibi. Haven't you tumbled to that? How do you know what he does after dropping you home? Peter may not be as good-looking as Luke, but I'll always come first with him. Luke's not the marrying kind and never will be!'

The next morning Gillian was gone, a note on her pillow saying she had eloped with Peter and would phone home when they arrived in Australia.

Andrea's stepmother had been heartbroken at her daughter's behaviour, and it had been left to Andrea to break the news of Gillian's departure to Luke.

Surprised to see her walk into his office at midday, he had greeted her with his usual warmth. That was one of the things she had liked about him. In spite of her age, he hadn't treated her like the skinny, spotty teenager she was, but as a young woman whose company he enjoyed.

'I—I'm sorry to bother you when you're working,' she had stammered.

'Forget it,' he had smiled. 'Why are you here? Did Gillian send you?'

'Not exactly. She's—er—she's gone away.'

'Gone away?'

'To Australia with a man called Peter Maynard,' Andrea had blurted out. 'They left today.'

There was a stunned silence, finally broken by Luke's saying softly, 'Would you mind repeating that?'

Andrea had, adding, 'She only told me yesterday, but I could see it coming for weeks. I wanted to warn you but—but I didn't have the courage.'

'So what gave you the courage now?' he had snapped.

'I—er—I felt it was the right thing to do. Gillian should have told you herself, but she—she didn't want a scene.'

'So her sweet baby sister is doing it for her!' Luke's face had contorted with fury. 'You're as two-faced as she is, fobbing me off every time I phoned from abroad. "Gillian's in bed with a migraine", "she's out with a girlfriend", "she's having dinner with Aunt Madge"! A tissue of lies, and you were part of it!'

'At least I've taken the trouble to come and tell you,' Andrea had defended herself.

'Worried in case there are no more free tickets to concerts?'

'If that's what you think, you can stick your tickets!' Andrea had cried and stormed out, vowing never to speak to him again.

A week later he had sent her a recording of Beethoven's Second Piano Concerto. 'A peace offering,' the accompanying note had said.

Angrily she had torn it up, thrown it into the wastepaper basket with the disc, and burst into tears. It was the last time she had cried over Luke, though she had retrieved the disc, which was still tucked away among a pile of others.

Had her crush on Luke affected her attitude to other men? she mused as the taxi turned into the tree-lined road where she lived; for though many men had wanted to share her life, she had only had a relationship with one: Roger Harrington, a British diplomat she had met at an embassy party in Paris, where she had gone to record a series of Chopin sonatas. There had been an instant mutual attraction. Could this be the one? she had questioned hopefully at the time, but had soon discovered that physical desire, enjoyable though it was, was insufficient basis for marriage. Sadly she had told him, and was deeply touched when he had asked if he could continue seeing her as a friend.

The taxi stopped outside her house and, as always, she felt a thrill of pleasure at sight of the gracious neo-Georgian façade and beautifully laid-out garden.

As she unlocked the front door she saw Mrs Prentice, her housekeeper, hovering in the hall.

'There's a visitor for you in the drawing-room,' she said.

'I'm not expecting anyone. Who is it?'

'A young woman. Said she knew you years ago.'

Andrea opened the drawing-room door and, as she did, the visitor turned from the window. The sun was behind her, placing her face in shadow, but as she moved, her face became visible: exquisitely cut features, and brown eyes that looked overly large in a too thin face.

'Gillian!' Andrea gasped.

'Annie!' her stepsister cried, and rushed towards her.

With a welcoming cry, Andrea clasped the slender figure close. 'Why didn't you let me know you were coming? And where have you been these past few months? I've tried phoning you but there was never any reply.'

'I've been away a lot. Holidays and things.'

'You look as if you can do with a holiday now,' Andrea couldn't help saying. 'You're bone-thin.'

'I'm fine. Fine.'

'How's Peter?' Andrea asked. She had only met him a couple of times—before he had eloped with Gillian—but had never blamed him for what had happened. How could she, when he hadn't known that Gillian was engaged to another man?

'I've left him,' her stepsister replied bluntly. 'Our marriage was a mistake.'

'But you kept saying in your letters how happy you were!'

'I was too proud to tell you the truth.'

'I see.' The coincidence of Gillian's coming back into her life the very day when she had seen Luke for the first time since her stepsister had ditched him struck Andrea as ironic.

'You don't seem awfully pleased to see me,' Gillian murmured.

'Of course I am. I'm surprised, that's all. You'll stay here, of course.'

'I was hoping you'd say that! Though I wasn't expecting anything as grand as this. You've certainly done well for yourself. Not that you don't deserve it. I read an article about you a few years ago, and it said you practised five hours a day. Is that true?'

'Sometimes I practise longer!' Andrea sat on the sofa, beckoning her stepsister to do the same. 'But don't let's talk about me. It's you I'm interested in. What went wrong between you and Peter?'

'The same thing that went wrong between Luke and myself.'

'You mean he was unfaithful too?'

'I don't know about that, but he had no time for me. Months would go by without us even having a meal together! He was at the office day and night and I was bored out of my skull. When I think of the glamorous life I could have led with Luke, I must have been crazy to give him up.'

'I wouldn't be so sure about that,' Andrea retorted. 'I doubt if Luke has changed his ways. Did Peter——?'

'I don't want to talk about him.' With a nervous gesture, Gillian pushed her hair away from her face. It was as thick and blonde as ever, but because she had lost weight it seemed too heavy for her slender neck. 'Tell me about you, Annie. Is there anyone special in *your* life, or is music your only love?'

'Let's say music doesn't leave me much time for anything else,' Andrea prevaricated, wondering if Gillian had bothered reading any of her letters, for she had written her at length about Roger Harrington.

'Playing the piano is no substitute for marriage,' Gillian said with a hint of scorn. 'You're nearly twenty-six, you know.'

'So what? At the moment I'm perfectly happy as I am.'

'You always were an odd kid. I remember you practising scales for hours on end. I suppose my engagement to Luke fuelled your ambition?'

'In a way,' Andrea murmured, unwilling to admit that it was his cruel rejection of her that had been the catalyst.

'I suppose that once you'd passed all your exams and training, he helped push your career.'

'Hardly!' Andrea exclaimed so vehemently that her stepsister looked startled. 'The only time I saw him was the day you ran off—when I went to tell him you'd gone. We had a blazing row and *I* walked out of his life too! I didn't write you about it because I didn't want to upset you.'

'If he took it out on you it was probably because he had a guilty conscience,' Gillian commented. 'Still, you made the big time without him, so it doesn't matter.' Brown eyes ranged the room. 'I can't get over how grand this place is, Annie—sorry, Andrea. Remember our old house near Epping Forest? We didn't have much money, but we were so happy together, even after your father died.'

Andrea nodded, warmed by memories. Her natural mother had been killed in a car accident soon after she was born, and a couple of years later her father had married Fay Brown, a young widow with an eight-year-old girl. Fay had taken little Annie to her heart, and though Gillian had tended to ignore her, it had only been because of the six-year age gap. Once Annie reached her early teens, Gillian had used her as a confidante. Of course, 'used' had been the operative word, her young stepsister had later realised with hindsight, but at the time she had been thrilled to be treated as an equal.

Family happiness had been shattered when Edgar Jones had died of a heart attack. He had been classics master at a private school, and while his insurance policy had ensured their financial security, there had been little money to spare for luxuries. But Fay had treated both girls as equals, and Andrea had always regarded her as the mother she had never known.

Gillian's elopement had hurt Fay, though the happy letters she received from her daughter had helped mitigate it. She had longed to visit her in Sydney, but Gillian, always promising to arrange it, did not do so until five years had passed. Then unexpectedly an aeroplane ticket had arrived for her—the very day she was going into hospital for a minor operation.

'I'll cancel it and have it done when I come back from Sydney,' Fay had said excitedly.

'It's better to have the op first,' Annie, now renamed Andrea and just setting out on her career, had suggested. 'You don't want to feel off colour while you're away.'

Fay had nodded. 'You're right, dear. And it's an open-date ticket, so I can go any time.'

Except that the time never came. Minor operation though it was, she had died under the anaesthetic, and Andrea, shattered by the loss, had been considering using the ticket herself—it would be good to be with her stepsister at this sad time—when Gillian had cabled her to return it so she could claim back the money on it.

In the years that had followed, news from Australia was sporadic, and though Andrea had done her best to maintain contact, it was an uphill task.

'It's as quiet here as it was at Epping Forest,' Gillian broke the silence as she walked over to the window and stared out at the uninterrupted view of Hampstead Heath.

'That's why I bought this house. It's rather isolated but I sometimes practise late at night, and if I had close neighbours they'd go berserk!'

'How many rooms are there?'

'Ten, plus a housekeeper's apartment.'

'You've really struck it rich, haven't you?' Brown eyes scanned the paintings on the walls, pausing at a small Chagall. 'That's real, isn't it?'

'Yes. A gift from the record company when I signed my second contract with them.'

'They must have made a fortune from the first one if this was their way of saying thank you!' Gillian lightly touched a jade figurine on the mantelshelf. 'Was this a gift too?'

'No. I bought it myself.' Sensing that the inquisition was going to continue, and mildly irritated by it, Andrea rose. 'Let me show you to your room. You must be jet lagged.'

Within minutes Gillian was flinging things out of her cases and strewing them round the beautiful bedroom suite she had been given.

'You haven't changed a bit,' Andrea smiled. 'You're as disorganised as ever.'

'*You've* changed completely in twelve years,' Gillian responded, untidily stacking the bathroom cabinet and marble shelves with toiletries. 'A pity we haven't seen each other for so long.'

'That wasn't my fault. Whenever I suggested flying out, you put me off.'

'Well, I'm here now, so we can catch up on what we've missed.' Gillian yawned and Andrea seized the chance of escaping, strangely reluctant to have a heart-to-heart with her stepsister.

'Why not have a rest first, Gilly? I'll ask Mrs Prentice to bring you a pot of coffee and some sandwiches. I don't have dinner until eight; that way I can get in some practice.'

'Suits me. I don't want to disturb your routine.'

Within minutes Andrea was at the piano, but was barely halfway through her practice when her stepsister came in.

'I hate being on my own,' Gillian apologised. 'Mind if I listen to you?'

'Not as long as you sit quietly.'

'I'll be quiet as a mouse.'

Andrea resumed her practice, but after a while Gillian started fidgeting, then rose and wandered the room, finally stopping beside the piano to stare at the slim white hands on the keyboard.

Doggedly Andrea tried to concentrate on the étude she was playing, knowing that in future she'd have to ban her sister from the room during these periods.

'Heavens, why am I bothering with this?' Abruptly she dropped her hands in her lap. 'It isn't every day my family drops in from the other side of the world! I'll go put some champagne on ice and tell Mrs Prentice we'll have dinner earlier.'

As if by magic, Gillian's restlessness vanished, and with a happy laugh she sank on to a sofa and tucked her legs beneath her. 'Champagne! That's the nicest word you've said since I arrived!'

They were both in a mellow mood when they sat facing each other across the highly polished dining table, and reminisced—sometimes happily, sometimes sadly—until they reached the coffee stage. Only then did Andrea refer again to Peter.

'Does he know where you are?'

'No. But I imagine he'll guess.'

'When did you decide to leave him?'

'When I'd reached breaking-point!'

No more was forthcoming, and Andrea swallowed her curiosity. Gillian had never been the reticent type, so perhaps there were details she found too painful to talk about. Either that, or she was still in love with Peter and didn't want to rubbish him.

'Just before I left Australia I read about Abraham Jessel's death,' Gillian said, diverting the conversation from herself. 'Who's going to be your manager now?'

It was a question Andrea had dreaded. 'Luke Kane, in fact—temporarily anyway. I hope to be free of him after my concert tour.'

'Luke? You're joking!'

'I wish I were. Abraham sold out to him, my contract included.' Andrea said nothing further. Bella's financial position was private and of no concern to anyone else.

'So now you're with Luke?' Gillian repeated. 'That must have been a shock for you.'

'For him too. Until I saw him this afternoon he had no idea Andrea Markham was Annie Jones. I suppose the change of name fooled him.'

'And your appearance. Anyone who hadn't seen you since you were a kid wouldn't recognise you today. You're so mature and serene.'

Gillian's tone gave Andrea the impression that she looked and dressed matronly.

'Abraham wanted me to project a particular image,' she said defensively.

'And it obviously paid off, so be thankful! But what about Luke? Is he as handsome as ever?'

Andrea hid her disquiet; was Gillian hankering after Luke again? 'He's thinner,' she answered slowly, 'and more controlled in his manner. But deep down he's still ambitious and ruthless.'

'Is he married?'

'No,' Andrea answered flatly.

'It will be interesting seeing him again. You'll be inviting him over, won't you?'

'Definitely not. He's no friend of mine, and after the way you treated him, I shouldn't think he's a friend of *yours*.'

'Oh, Annie, that's all water under the bridge. I'm sure Luke's forgotten it by now. I know I have.'

'You weren't the one who was jilted.'

'He deserved to be.'

'Then why on earth do you want to see him again?'

'Because he may be different today. I know *I* am.'

'That's true. You're a married woman.'

'Who has left her husband and regards herself as free.'

Andrea was disconcerted. 'I'm sorry. I didn't realise a divorce was in the offing.'

With a shrug, Gillian pushed back her chair and led the way into the living-room, where she instantly curled up in a corner of the sofa and made herself comfortable. She had changed into a housecoat before dinner, and her soft blonde hair shone against the pale blue brocade, its soft folds disguising her thin frame.

She was still very pretty and knew it, Andrea reflected, and might well try to get things going again with Luke. Somehow she couldn't see his succumbing to Gillian's charms a second time, though she wouldn't put it past him to lead her stepsister on and then walk out on her—as she had done to him! The thought was worrying. There was a brittleness about Gillian that disturbed her; as if it would take very little to send her over the edge and into a breakdown.

'I'm surprised you still dislike Luke,' Gillian said unexpectedly. 'I mean, your quarrel with him was a silly one. He was furious with me and he took it out on you—which is understandable. So for heaven's sake act like an adult and forget it.'

It was the voice of reason, but Andrea's antipathy towards Luke had nothing to do with reason. It was instinctive.

'On the other hand,' Gillian went on, 'I'm glad you're no longer starry-eyed about him. It would be awkward if we both fancied him!' A dreamy look came over her face. 'Deep down I think I've always loved him.'

Andrea's heart sank. 'Aren't you romanticising? As I recollect it, you fell for Peter the first time you met him.'

'Because I was angry with Luke.'

'And now you're ready to take up with him again because you're angry with your husband!'

'I suppose you think I don't know my own mind?' Gillian said sulkily.

'Let's say I think you're confused,' Andrea replied.

'I'm just the opposite. What I said proves how consistent I am in my affections.'

It was said so seriously, yet was manifestly so ridiculous that Andrea burst out laughing. Gillian looked momentarily hurt, then unexpectedly grinned.

'It's good to talk to somebody frankly, Annie. I couldn't have such a heart-to-heart with Peter.'

'That's hardly surprising!'

'Did Luke ask about me today?'

'No.'

'That means he's still hurt.'

'Or else that you don't mean anything to him.'

'If that were true he'd have asked about me out of politeness. No, I'm sure he still cares.'

Andrea marvelled at Gillian's conceit; it was an aspect of her character that had not changed.

'If you won't fix up for me to meet Luke, I'll do it myself,' her stepsister went on, rising and moving towards the door. 'I'm off to bed. I'm so tired I won't need any sleeping-pills tonight.'

'Do you often take them?'

Silk-clad shoulders lifted in a shrug. 'Goodnight, baby sister! See you in the morning.'

Andrea murmured goodnight, then settled back in her chair, still disquieted by a strangeness in Gillian's behaviour that she could not pin-point. Or was it that the two of them had drifted apart? After all, twelve years was a long time not to see anyone.

CHAPTER THREE

ANDREA had a restless night, her mind teeming with thoughts of Luke and her stepsister. It had been foolish of her to refuse to arrange a meeting, for it would make Gillian more determined to see him. People were perverse. Luke for example, where she herself was concerned. A man who had the pick of the world's musical talent should have let her go gracefully, but the more she had shown her dislike of him, the stronger he had fought to retain her.

But then Luke had never done the expected. Perhaps it had something to do with his unconventional background—or at least unconventional for a classical music impresario. His father had been a foreman at a car plant, and his mother a cook in the staff canteen of the same company. Luke had gone to the local school but at seventeen had won a scholarship to Oxford, where he had taken an engineering degree, clearly influenced by his father.

It had proved a short-lived career, for within a year, after a chance meeting with Abraham Jessel, he had taken the quantum leap from engineering to music. It had been a back-breaking effort to prove himself but he had done brilliantly.

Since Gillian had left him his name had been linked with many lovely, talented women, but none had succeeded in leading him to the altar. Perhaps the pressures of his profession ruled out marriage, for it was tough to stay at the top and, from what she remembered of him, he was nothing if not single-minded in his ambition.

Next morning she decided to apprise him of her stepsister's return to London, and, not giving herself time to change her mind, telephoned to find out when he was free.

'Mr Kane is always free to see you,' his secretary said, which made her suspect he had given specific instructions that he was always available to her. Talk about buttering up fractious clients! 'Is eleven convenient, Miss Markham?'

'Eleven is fine.'

She was finishing her breakfast when Gillian sauntered into the dining-room, her thinness evident in the catsuit she sported.

'You're up early,' Andrea smiled. 'You never used to surface till noon unless you had to go to work!'

'I haven't been sleeping well lately,' Gillian confessed. 'By the way, I want to see a doctor. I've run out of sleeping-pills.'

'My GP won't prescribe them unless they're absolutely necessary.'

'I wouldn't be taking them if they weren't! But my other pills have upset my sleeping pattern.'

Andrea's earlier anxiety about her stepsister returned. 'What other pills?'

'Oh, something for depression,' Gillian answered vaguely.

'How long have——?'

'What a delicious smell of coffee,' Gillian deliberately interrupted, and prattled on brightly as she poured herself a cup and nibbled on some toast, crumbling most of it on her plate. 'I'm still not a breakfast-eater,' she joked 'Remember how cross Mother used to get with me?'

Andrea smiled. 'I always promised myself that if ever I had children, I'd never nag them because they weren't eating enough.'

'I couldn't agree more.'

'A pity you don't have a family. It might have helped keep you and Peter together.'

Gillian's face flamed. 'Who needs children?' she shouted. 'They cause nothing but problems. My marriage is finished and I don't want to discuss it. If I'd known you were going to keep prying like this, I'd never have come here. I—I——' She choked on her words and burst into tears.

'Darling, don't! I wasn't prying. I was simply making conversation.' Dismayed by the hysterical outburst, Andrea was convinced Gillian was teetering on the edge of a nervous breakdown. 'I'll ring Dr Marshall before I leave and ask him to come to see you.'

'Leave? Where are you going?' Gillian asked anxiously, keeping her face averted.

'I have a business appointment. I'll see you later.'

Precisely at eleven, Andrea was ushered into Luke's office.

'It's a pleasure to see you again so soon.' He came forward to greet her, handsome yet menacing in an Armani charcoal shirt with matching cotton trousers and plaited black leather belt. They emphasised his height and leanness, and set off his lightly tanned skin.

Her breath caught in her throat—he was so damned handsome. Her schoolgirl crush on him, which she had believed dead, was resuscitating itself into something stronger and far more adult.

'This isn't a social call,' she stated, her voice trembling slightly. 'I came to tell you Gillian's back. She arrived unexpectedly yesterday afternoon. Her marriage is over and she's staying with me.'

If the news came as a shock to him, he didn't show it. 'Is that why you're here? Because of Gillian?'

'I thought it might embarrass you to go on representing me.'

His burst of laughter was genuine. 'Do you think I'm carrying a torch for her?' He shook his head. 'I haven't been living like a monk for the past twelve years, you know.'

'I didn't imagine you had,' Andrea replied chillingly.

'Then why are you here? No, let me guess. You think I'll release you from your contract rather than run the risk of meeting her?'

'It might save you embarrassment. I know you were hurt and——'

'It won't embarrass me,' he interrupted. 'And I doubt if it will embarrass your sister. *You're* the one who hasn't forgotten the past. If you could, we'd be friends.'

Aware he had made her appear foolish, she rose to leave.

'What are you scared of?' he challenged, barring her way. 'That I might fall for Gillian again?'

'Or she for you,' Andrea retorted. 'And I don't want her hurt.'

'She's a big girl, *Annie*. She can take care of herself.'

His mocking expression made Andrea feel even more stupid for coming here. 'Why can't you release me?' she bit out. 'You've plenty of other money-spinners on your books. I can't be all that important to you.'

'But you *are.*' He looked her full in the face. 'I was listening to some of your recordings last night, and I believe that one day you could be the greatest pianist in the world.'

'You mean I'm not already?' she mocked.

'Not quite. Your playing needs a little more passion. Perhaps when you have it in your life, it will appear in your music.'

Andrea's breath caught in her throat. The nerve of him! 'You don't know a damned thing about my private life! How dare——?'

'I dare because I believe in you.'

Silently she stalked out, conscious of his walking beside her to the lift.

'Remember me to Gillian,' he said, 'and say I'm looking forward to seeing her.'

'You really mean that, don't you?'

He shrugged. 'I just told you I don't give a damn about the past.'

'From what the papers say, you don't give a damn for any woman either!'

'If you accept everything the tabloids say, then *you* are a frigid female interested only in your career!'

Hoist with her own petard, Andrea's recourse was to exit smartly, and as the lift door opened, that was precisely what she did. Unfortunately, Luke's foot stopped it from closing.

'Are you afraid of having me as your manager because of my reputation with women?' he asked quietly.

'You flatter yourself! I find you completely resistible!'

'Pity,' he drawled as he moved his foot away. 'I find *you* irresistible!'

The door closed before she could conjure up a scathing remark, and she was seething with temper as she hailed a taxi. She dreaded her coming tour. Not only would she have to hide her terror of crowds from Luke—a man of his temperament would have little patience with phobias—but also contend with his disturbing presence.

'I've *got* to cope,' she muttered, bitterly acknowledging that it wasn't only her fear of crowds that was the problem. It was her fear of Luke. Her body tingled at sight of him and she knew an insane longing to touch him, to see if his skin felt as smooth as it looked, his hair as silky. Her stomach lurched in panic. No man had affected her so strongly, and it was imperative she break with him as soon as the tour ended.

She was walking up the drive to her house when Dr Marshall came down the steps.

'Glad you caught me,' he greeted her warmly. 'I've had a long talk with your sister.'

'What's the matter with her, Dr Marshall?'

'She's severely depressed.'

'Severely?'

'Yes. She's on strong antidepressants, so they're masking some of the symptoms. Tell me, how well do you know her husband?'

'I only met him a few times, but he seemed nice enough. Until she arrived here I had no idea she wasn't happy with him.'

The doctor opened the door of his car. 'I'll drop by later in the week. She wouldn't give me the name of her doctor—said he was on a sabbatical—otherwise I'd call him.'

Andrea's unease grew. 'Don't hold anything back from me. If Gillian's seriously ill, I want to know.'

'There's no cause for alarm at the moment. But it's important that she isn't left on her own to brood.'

'That won't be easy! From what she said last night, she's lost touch with her old friends and wouldn't want to see them anyway.'

'So that puts the onus on *you*,' came the sympathetic comment.

Andrea nodded. 'And very awkward it is too. I've a concert tour in the offing and that means a very heavy work-load.'

'All the more reason to take time off. Everyone needs to relax occasionally.'

'*I* don't,' Andrea assured him with a smile as he climbed behind the wheel. 'All *I* need is music.'

Even as she spoke, she knew she was lying. It might have been true a couple of days ago, but not any longer. Keeping the smile fixed on her face, she entered the house.

Gillian, standing by the telephone in the hall, swung round guiltily. 'Hello, Andrea. I—I've asked Luke to dinner tomorrow night.'

'Here?' Andrea was appalled.

'Why not? I thought if I—if we all met socially you'd get back on your old footing with him. I know you said he's only managing you for this tour, but it would make things easier for you if you could at least be friendly with him.'

Andrea was angry, knowing it wasn't *her* interests Gillian had at heart, but, mindful of Dr Marshall's injunction, she made herself nod.

'Perhaps you're right, Gilly. But next time check with me before inviting anyone here.'

Tears filled the brown eyes. 'I'm sorry. I thought you'd want me to feel at home.'

'Darling, I do. I didn't mean it the way it sounded. But to be honest, I'm feeling my nerves are frazzled at the moment, and I don't want to do any entertaining. Losing Abraham has upset me.'

'Then I'm glad I'm here to keep you company. You need to get out of yourself and stop moping. As soon as I feel a bit brighter, why don't we throw a party?'

'Perhaps we will,' Andrea murmured, aware that if she weren't careful, Gillian would be running her life. Once her sister was better, she'd have to tactfully indicate that staying here couldn't be a permanent arrangement, even if she had to subsidise the move.

'Luke said he saw you this morning.' Gillian was speaking again. 'You didn't go to warn him I was here, did you?'

'I went to discuss my tour,' Andrea lied. 'I can't bear the thought of performing before a live audience.'

'You mean you're still scared of being surrounded by people?' Gillian gave a nervous laugh. 'But does it matter? You've made a fortune from your recordings.'

Andrea remained silent. Was money the only thing her stepsister appreciated?

'I suppose you blame me for your phobia?' Gillian went on. 'But nothing terrible happened to you in the park that day, and——'

'I don't *know* what happened,' Andrea almost shouted. 'That's what's so terrible. *I can't remember.* I've tried and tried but my mind's a blank. Just those dreadful boys surrounding me and—and...' She turned away, fighting for control. 'Let's not talk about it.'

'Maybe you should!'

'No!' Vainly Andrea tried to suppress the horror welling up in her as the past came vividly to life. She had been eight at the time, and Gillian a flirtatious fourteen-year-old who had wanted to go boating on the lake with a boy from her school.

'I'll only be gone half an hour,' she had promised. 'You'll be fine in the playground.'

To begin with Andrea had enjoyed playing with another little girl. But then the child went home and she was left by herself. Shortly afterwards a group of teenage boys came strolling by and started teasing her. Her obvious fear spurred them on and they surrounded her, jeering and laughing as she started to cry.

One boy grabbed hold of her and the others closed in around her. Even now, seventeen years later, she could not recall precisely what had happened next. All she remembered was that her hysterical screams eventually caught the attention of a woman passerby, who started shouting and calling 'Police!' The youths ran off and the woman had comforted her as best she could, and asked where she lived.

Before Andrea could tell her, Gillian had returned, and the woman had rounded on her angrily for leaving her young sister alone. Scared and guilty, Gillian had grabbed Andrea's hand and run out of the park, not stopping until they had left the woman far behind. Only then had she come to a halt and made Andrea swear not to say anything to their parents. Tearfully Andrea had agreed; in those days she would have walked on hot coals to please her stepsister.

For weeks afterwards, her sleep had been disturbed by nightmares she was unable to recall, and not being able to confide her fears to her parents had made them far worse. They had continued for several years, but as they decreased in intensity, she developed a fear of crowds. She would panic in busy stores or the cinema, and have to be brought home by taxi rather than bus or train.

Yet strangely, giving concerts at school had presented no problems, nor had playing in piano competitions. But her terror had returned when, as a professional, she had given her first public performance, and ten minutes after the start of the 'Emperor' Concerto, she had run from the stage of the Festival Hall and refused to return.

Certain that the incident in the park was responsible for her phobia, she had consulted a psychiatrist, but months of dialogue had failed to resolve her problem, and she decided not to give any further public performances.

Despite this she became internationally renowned through her record albums and the occasional TV show, though here too, no audience was present. It was Abraham who finally pressured her into agreeing to do a short series of public concerts, though she had never imagined that when the time came for her to do them he wouldn't be by her side.

'If you hate crowds, cancel the tour.' Gillian's comment returned her to the present.

'I can't. There are obligations, financial commitments.' Anxious to cut short the conversation, she opened the music-room door. 'I have to practise. If you'll excuse me . . .'

'I'll come and sit with you.'

'I'm sorry, but you can't. You keep fidgeting and it disturbs me.'

'I'll be quiet as a mouse.'

'That's what you said yesterday, but you weren't.'

'Oh, very well.' With an angry swish of skirt, Gillian flounced upstairs. 'I'm going to my room to read,' she called over her shoulder. 'If you're bothered by me turning the pages of *Vogue*, bang on the ceiling!'

CHAPTER FOUR

NEXT day, Luke's impending visit loomed so large on Andrea's horizon that she was filled with gloom. It was bad enough having to meet him in his office, but entertaining him in the intimacy of her home would leave her with memories that would be far harder to eradicate.

She tried to shut him out of her mind by practising, but found it so difficult to concentrate that she kept leaving the piano either to make unimportant telephone calls, or have another cup of coffee.

Gillian, for her part, was in top form, which gave Andrea a grain of comfort, and spent the day bustling round, getting things ready. Just like a young girl preparing to entertain her lover, she made sure the vases were filled with blooms from the garden, insisted on laying the table herself, and ran to and fro from the kitchen to supervise Mrs Prentice—who was a cordon bleu cook but diplomatically held her tongue.

Eventually Andrea gave up any attempt to work and went to her room to select something to wear for the evening. After some consideration she settled on a black silk crêpe double-breasted jacket with matching high-waisted trousers and a cream silk blouse that she had bought for a recent dinner party given by the producer of her last television show. It had a Spanish look that suited her dark beauty and would, she reflected, be a suitable foil for Gillian, who was bound to choose an outfit to highlight her blonde good looks.

This was confirmed when Gillian entered the drawing-room at seven-thirty, in a shirt-waister dress in pale blue cotton piqué. The see-through top was in fine georgette, through which one glimpsed a lacy flesh-coloured bra and silky skin, while the hip-hugging, well above-knee skirt drew attention to her incredibly long legs.

'I can't wait to see Luke,' she gushed, drifting round the room. 'How do I look? I wonder what he'll think of me?'

'He'll think you're lovelier than ever,' Andrea remarked, sensitive to her stepsister's desperate need for approval.

'Honestly? Sometimes I think I look an absolute hag.'

'Nonsense. You don't look a day older than I do.'

Gillian patted her hair. 'They say dark people always look older than fair ones, and your hairstyle doesn't help either. You should cut it short—that bun is ageing.'

'It's not a bun, it's a loose knot,' Andrea said good-humouredly. 'And I think it makes me look dramatic.'

'It also makes you look severe and efficient. You should try the little-girl-lost look. Men prefer it.'

The doorbell forestalled Andrea's answer, and with an excited cry of 'He's here!' Gillian rushed to open the drawing-room door.

Andrea felt as if she was watching a mini-drama unfold. As Luke came in, Gillian held out her hands to him in a pleading gesture, and he surveyed her in silence, hands motionless at his sides, face calm but not unfriendly. Then he moved forward and took both her hands.

'Gillian! You haven't changed a bit.' Lightly he kissed first one cheek, then the other.

'Flatterer!' she smiled, fluttering her eyelashes.

He smiled back. 'Surely you remember I never say things I don't mean?'

'Can I take it that you forgive me, then, in spite of the way I behaved?'

'Harbouring bitterness only corrodes oneself, Gilly. I forgave you long ago.'

As he spoke his gaze went to Andrea, as if wanting her to note what he had said, and she was conscious of the colour coming into her cheeks as he walked over to her. His single-breasted jacket—mushroom corduroy and matching his trousers, which were belted in tan leather—was instantly recognisable as Paul Smith, and were complemented by a mushroom silk sweater, and she grudgingly conceded how well the smartly casual look suited his whipcord leanness.

'Thank you for inviting me to your home,' he said so softly that only she could hear.

'My sister invited you.'

Luke's eyes glinted. 'I had hoped *you* were handing me an olive branch!'

'Will you release me from my contract?' she countered smoothly.

'I thought we'd settled that matter!'

Andrea flushed, but kept her temper; he was, after all, a guest in her home.

Gillian came over and linked her arm through his. 'What do you think of my little sister now?' she quipped. 'I bet you never guessed twelve years ago that one day you'd be her manager!'

'I'd never heard her play, so I had no idea of her potential.'

'You knew I passed all my music exams with honours,' Andrea couldn't help saying. 'You just weren't interested.'

'Many youngsters do well in exams, but very few go on to develop as you did. I made a big mistake and I deeply regret it. But I shall make up for it by taking special care of you.'

'Let's stop talking about the past and have a drink,' Gillian suggested brightly. 'Will you open the champagne, Luke?'

'Of course.'

Watching him as he deftly uncorked the bottle, poured the foaming liquid into the fluted goblets and passed them round, Andrea was dismayed by her body's reaction to his masculinity. Her nipples stiffened and she was thankful that her black crêpe jacket hid them from sight, though as Luke's silver-grey eyes met hers she was hard put to it not to fold her arms across her chest.

'You have a delightful home,' he commented, settling into a chair by the window. 'I envy you the quiet and greenery.'

'Where do *you* live?' Gillian asked.

'I've an apartment above my office in Mayfair.'

'If you want quiet and greenery,' Andrea put in, 'what keeps you in central London?'

'Convenience. I do most of my entertaining in town.'

'I hope your offices are smarter than the two scruffy rooms you had when you first started?'

'Those were tough times,' Luke agreed with feeling. 'I'm not sure I'd have the courage to go through all that again.'

Had success spoilt and softened him? Andrea wondered as she listened.

'Money brings self-indulgence,' he went on, perhaps guessing her thoughts. 'I now like things to come easily to me.'

'You mean you aren't a fighter any more?' Andrea questioned, her voice palpably disbelieving.

'Let's say I'm more choosy about what I fight for.'

'The choice being dependent on the money it brings you, I suppose?'

For the briefest instant anger flared in his eyes, turning the grey to silver. 'Rarely, these days, my dear. I'm more inclined to choose what pleasures me.'

Andrea swallowed hard. He wasn't suggesting... She was considering what to say when Gillian made a reply unnecessary.

'I wish you could be *my* manager, Luke!'

'I shouldn't think any man could manage you!' he teased. 'You always did as you wanted.'

'And I was so often wrong.' She leaned towards him imploringly. 'I behaved so badly with you—running off without a word.'

'Forget it,' he smiled. 'The way I look at it, you gave me twelve extra years of freedom!'

Gillian laughed, composure regained. 'You speak as if your freedom's coming to an end!'

The raising of a black eyebrow was his only reply, and much to Andrea's relief, Mrs Prentice came in to say dinner was ready.

Gillian immediately hurried out, murmuring that she was going to the kitchen. Andrea met her housekeeper's surprised gaze and hid a smile, knowing her stepsister's show of domesticity was aimed at impressing Luke.

Amazingly enough he was taken in, for he compli-
mented her on the *escalopes de veau Roquefort* as soon
as he had had a few mouthfuls.

'I remembered it was one of your favourites,' she
confided, and modestly looked down at her hands.

'Mrs Prentice is a marvellous cook,' Andrea heard
herself say, and was instantly ashamed of her bitchi-
ness. If Gillian was intent on ensnaring Luke again—
and her behaviour tonight suggested it—who was she to
object? He was eligible on every count, and his glamorous lifestyle would hold enormous appeal, given her
stepsister's discontent with living in Australia. Andrea
glanced at Luke's hard, chiselled features. Surely he was
too intelligent to be happy with a woman who, though
not quite the epitome of the dumb blonde, was definitely lightweight? Yet clever men often preferred their
women dumb; it probably helped them relax.

'Come back, Andrea,' Luke said.

'What?' With a start she realised he was speaking to
her. 'I—er—what did you say?'

'I said come back. You were clearly miles away.'

He should only know how close to home she was!

'I bet you were thinking of the tour,' Gillian said,
anxious to get into the conversation. 'When does it begin?'

'Too soon,' Andrea answered, stabbing her fork into
a potato.

'Not for me. I can't wait to see Rome.'

'I didn't realise you were going with your sister,' Luke
said, not seeming to notice the startled look on Andrea's
face.

'She needs me for moral support,' Gillian pronounced. 'And for company too—strange cities can be
pretty lonely.'

'Lonely is the last thing I'll be!' Andrea asserted.

'You'll be among people, sure, but that's not the same as having somebody close to you to help with any problems.'

Andrea did not relish the prospect of relying on Gillian who, with her restlessness and constant chatter, was likely to cause more problems than solve them. 'You might find the pace a bit hectic,' she murmured.

'I'll love it!' The blonde head tilted in Luke's direction. 'I hope you'll come to Rome to see us?'

His mouth curved upwards. 'I'll be with Andrea throughout the tour.'

This was news to Andrea, and if she hadn't just set down her fork, she would certainly have dropped it. 'That's quite unnecessary,' she said through clenched teeth.

'When possible it's a service I provide for many of my solo clients,' he assured her.

'Well, this is one client who doesn't require it.'

'When Abraham mentioned your tour he told me he was going to accompany you, so I intend doing the same.'

'You don't mind *my* being there do you, Luke?' Gillian interposed eagerly.

'Not if you contribute to your sister's peace of mind.'

If this wasn't the answer hoped for, Gillian was too shrewd to show it and glanced at him coquettishly. He favoured her with a grin, and Andrea would have given a great deal to read his mind. Was he putting on an act with her stepsister because he thought it might help him retain a commercially valuable client, or was he genuinely falling for her again?

She was relieved when dinner was ended and they could return to the drawing-room, where she sat as far from Luke as possible.

'Do you still drink Turkish?' Gillian asked him and, at his nod, hurried out.

'You must be delighted to have Gillian with you again,' he said conversationally.

Andrea shrugged. 'I'm not sure.'

'That's a surprising answer.'

'It's an honest one at least.'

'Pity you weren't always so honest.'

Anger turned her violet eyes to indigo. 'I knew it! You still haven't forgiven me for not telling you Gillian was dating Peter?'

'Let's say I remember how disappointed I was in you.'

'Because I felt I owed my loyalty to my sister, not you?' She almost admitted the misery and soul-seeking it had caused her to be a helpless party to the deceit, but refused to give him that satisfaction. What irony that he should forgive Gillian but not herself! Tears pricked her lids and, afraid he might see them, she rose and went to the window on the pretext of drawing the curtains.

'Please leave them,' he said. 'I like seeing the night sky.'

She dropped her hands but remained irresolute, gazing outside.

'I'm sorry if I upset you,' he remarked, coming to stand behind her.

Speechlessly she went on staring at the garden. Damn him for being so sensitive to her thoughts! But she had to counter his belief; it was important to her pride.

'I wasn't upset. Merely irritated that you seem able to forgive Gillian, yet still hold a grudge against *me*.'

'Because I *expected* more from you.'

'Why? *I* wasn't your fiancée, for heaven's sake!'

'I know.' His voice was clipped. 'I guess emotions aren't always logical. But you're right about one thing. I should have known that a kid as caring and sensitive as you were would put family loyalty above everything else. So will you forgive me and let the past go?'

Andrea turned slowly to face him. She had no choice but to accept his apology, though it would make no difference to her determination to be rid of him as her manager. If she didn't, she would end up as one more scalp on his belt. But her thoughts were not evident in her voice as she spoke.

'I forgive you, Luke.'

'Good.' His hand came out and caressed the side of her cheek. Instinctively she drew back and he regarded her quizzically. 'What's wrong?'

'Nothing. I don't like being touched.'

'By anyone, or just me?'

Without answering she returned to her chair. 'Gillian must have gone to Turkey to fetch the coffee beans!' she said lightly.

'I'm in no hurry.'

'Do you find her changed?'

'It's hard to say. *I've* changed, and that's altered my perception. She's prettier than I remember, and she struck me as nervous and tense. Par for the course, I guess, if your marriage breaks up.' He paused to eye a Vlaminck above the mantelpiece. 'This painting reminds me of you.' He waved a hand at the green and brown blobs that, if one stood sufficiently far away, resolved themselves into twisted, rippling trees swayed by a fierce wind.

Seeing his swift change of subject as a sign that he did not wish to discuss his ex-fiancée, Andrea went along with it.

'I don't think I'm flattered!' she said.

'Why not? It's striking and mysterious. I find you an enigma, which is something I hadn't anticipated.'

'Why? Because you knew me when I was thirteen? Teenagers change, you know.'

'But you were always spontaneous and fiery. That can't have disappeared.'

'It's gone into my music.'

'You should let some into your life.' His voice was deep, intimate, and he moved a step closer to her. 'You're too controlled, too serious for your age. What are you afraid of, Andrea—living?'

'Don't be presumptuous,' she said icily. 'You know nothing about me.'

'I'm hoping that will change.'

'Not if I have anything to do with it.'

His eyes glinted. 'Maybe we're both wary of having our armour penetrated.' He paused, as if waiting for her to comment, and when she didn't, said, 'Whether you want it to happen or not, we'll know considerably more about each other before your tour is over.'

'Possibly. But since I don't anticipate seeing you again after it, it won't matter to me.'

With easy grace he resumed his seat, making no attempt to sit nearer to her. 'I'm pleased Gillian will be travelling with you.' He reverted to their original topic. 'It's better for her to be occupied while she's getting over her divorce.'

That her stepsister was divorced was news to Andrea. She had had the impression Gillian had only just left her husband. Had she lied to Luke, to make him think she was available?

'Coffee!' Gillian announced cheerfully, coming in with a tray.

'I'll take mine to my room,' Andrea said as she accepted a cup. 'You and Luke must have reams to talk about.'

Neither of them objected, and she was ruefully reminded that this was the same way she had acted years ago when Luke had come to the house to see her stepsister. Talk about the clock turning full cycle!

Her foot was on the first stair when Luke softly spoke her name, and she turned to see that he had followed her into the hall.

'I hope you aren't going to your room because I'm here?' he challenged.

'Oh, dear,' she responded, flippant to cover her embarrassment. 'And there was I, trying so hard to make you feel wanted!'

His mouth thinned. 'Black suits you, Andrea. Reflects your sense of humour.'

'I dress to please myself. Not a man.'

'That's what's missing from your life: a man to dress—and undress—for.'

Head high, she looked at him, 'If you're thinking of offering your services, forget it. I don't go in for other women's rejects.'

His jaw jutted forward as he clenched it. 'And I never mix business with pleasure, so we both know exactly where we stand!'

Turning on his heels, he strode into the drawing-room, leaving Andrea to climb the stairs, the happy sound of Gillian's laughter, and Luke's husky response, echoing in her ears.

CHAPTER FIVE

ANDREA was still awake at one o'clock when Luke's car drove off. A few moments later her bedroom door opened slightly and she heard Gillian whisper, 'Are you still awake, Annie?'

Andrea remained quiet as a mouse, breathing a sigh of relief as the door closed. The last thing she wanted was an exchange of girlish confidences about Luke! Despite his flattering remarks about her talent, and his subtle flirtatiousness, he made her feel inadequate as a woman; implied she had yet to experience what sex was all about. God, did it show that clearly?

Passionate though she was in her emotions, her affair with Roger had roused no spark in her. Yet she could not lay the blame at his door, for he was a man of considerable experience, and ever since she had been plagued by the fear that she was sexually frigid.

Her thoughts reverted to Luke and she imagined his lean, strong body, muscles rippling beneath the tanned skin, bearing down on her, his devouring mouth and wandering hands arousing sensations she had never before experienced. With a moan she buried her face in her pillow, longing for the oblivion of sleep.

At nine next morning Gillian awoke her with a cup of coffee. 'Luke called you a short while ago.' She perched on the bed in her flower-sprigged dressing-gown and reached for the telephone. 'Shall I get him for you?'

'No!' Andrea said sharply. 'I'll call him later.'

'It was great seeing him again,' Gillian went on. 'I was mad to have left him.'

'He gave you good reason!' Andrea reminded her.

Gillian pulled a face. 'I'd be more broad-minded today! Luke's so devastating, you can't blame women throwing themselves at him. I'd marry him tomorrow, given the chance.'

'I assumed you were still married to Peter,' Andrea remarked, 'though I gather you told Luke you were already divorced.'

Gillian went scarlet. 'I said my marriage was over. He must have misunderstood me.'

'I doubt if he's the type to do that. So if you're hoping to have a serious relationship with him, don't base it on a lie.'

'It isn't a lie! I *am* going to divorce Peter. I've plenty of grounds.'

Andrea sipped her coffee. 'Tell me about it, Gilly. You never have.'

'Because I can't bear thinking about it!' Gillian jumped up and paced the carpet. 'You've no idea how cruel he was! So jealous that I had to tell him where I was every minute of the day. He even had me followed!'

Her voice rose and she started shaking, and Andrea pushed aside the duvet and ran over to her. If proof were needed that her sister was ill, she had it now.

'Come and lie down,' she murmured, gently leading her to her bedroom across the hall.

'I want a tranquilliser,' Gillian gasped, waving a hand vaguely in the direction of her bathroom, and Andrea went in search of one. She was dismayed by the daunting array of medication and made a mental note to tell

Dr Marshall. Filling a glass with water, she gave her sister the pill she had asked for, and stayed with her until she started to drowse.

This latest outburst had made it abundantly clear that Gillian's depression was connected with her marriage and, given this, perhaps the sooner she was divorced the better. But what if it led to her eventually marrying Luke? Andrea pushed the thought aside and forced herself to return his call.

'Two things,' he said as he came on the line, his voice quick, vibrant. 'To thank you for last night, and to discuss your clothes.'

'My *what*?'

'The clothes for your tour.'

'I've already bought two new evening dresses, and I have several others I've only worn once for video recordings.'

'I've seen them—I ran through all your tapes—and they won't do.'

'They come from one of the top designers in the country!'

'They're lovely,' he said equably, 'but they don't project the image I want for you.'

'I like my image.'

'Your contract gives me the right to approve it.'

Andrea knew this to be true, but once Abraham had effected her original transformation, he had never invoked this power again, allowing her free rein and often complimenting her on her dress sense. Yet it appeared one man's meat was another man's poison. For the moment Luke held all the cards and it was sensible to give in with good grace.

'If you tell me the image you have in mind, I'll go and——'

'I intend supervising your wardrobe myself,' he cut across her. 'I've fixed for us to see Hilary Dix this afternoon, if that's convenient.'

In spite of her good intentions, Andrea had difficulty controlling her temper. Apart from resenting being treated like a frump, Hilary Dix had a tremendous 'showbiz' following and was known for her flamboyantly sexy creations. It looked as if her worst fears about the way Luke proposed promoting her were about to be realised.

'You'll like Hilary,' he said into the silence. 'She's fun.'

'Shopping for clothes can never be fun. It's a boring but necessary evil.'

'I promise you'll find shopping with me fun,' he said, ignoring her comment. 'I'll meet you at Hilary's at two-thirty, or earlier if you'll have lunch with me?'

'If I'm out this afternoon I should practise this morning,' she excused.

'See you later, then.'

Distinctly ruffled that he had not pressed her to change her mind, Andrea showered and slipped into a tracksuit before going down to practise. It was one o'clock before she stopped for a light lunch. Gillian joined her, and seemed to have completely recovered.

'Are you practising this afternoon as well?' she asked.

'No. I'm meeting Luke at Hilary Dix's, to choose some clothes for my concerts.'

'Wow! She's one of my favourite designers. May I come with you?'

Andrea knew it was more a desire to see Luke again than the couturier that was behind the request. But it saved her from being the only focus of his attention, though it meant putting up with Gillian's flirtatiousness.

'By all means come,' she answered. 'I'm meeting him there at two-thirty.'

'I'll go and change,' Gillian said, and dashed out.

She reappeared as the taxi arrived, looking so pretty in an ice-pink two-piece that Andrea felt like a dull sparrow in her beige silk suit.

'This is old,' Gillian lamented when Andrea admired her outfit. 'I haven't bought anything new for ages.'

'If you see anything you fancy today, I'll get it for you.'

'Oh, Annie!' Gillian hugged her. 'I'm so glad you're successful and rich. I'm not envious, just awfully proud of you.'

Andrea hugged her back, knowing she spoke the truth; for all her sister's faults, jealousy was not one of them.

Luke was already in the Knightsbridge showroom chatting to the couturier when they arrived. She was in her late thirties, her appearance as eye-catching as that of her most flamboyant clients, which did little to assuage Andrea's foreboding.

'I'm delighted to have the opportunity of dressing you,' the woman beamed. 'Luke has already selected several outfits for you to try on. I've put them in a dressing-room, but I can have them modelled for you first if you prefer?'

'That won't be necessary,' Andrea replied, anxious to make this shopping expedition as short as possible.

Did Luke bring all his younger artists here, and his girlfriends too? she wondered as she went into the small but well appointed changing-room. Most likely both.

He was on first-name terms with Hilary Dix, so they clearly had more than a passing acquaintance.

Annoyingly, she discovered she liked Luke's taste in clothes and, contrary to her fears, he had chosen the least bizarre creations. Even so, they were way-out compared with anything else in her wardrobe, and it was with some trepidation that she stepped into the first outfit: a beautifully cut halter-top in hot-pink silk, with a hot-pink and tangerine silk wrap skirt.

She barely recognised herself, so dramatic was the change to her personality. From temperate to temptress, she thought, seeing how the tropical colours emphasised the blackness of her hair, which in turn drew attention to the purity of her creamy skin. Talk about Tondaleo of the South Seas!

There was a knock on the door, and the couturier walked in.

'Stunning,' she pronounced. 'You have the right colouring and figure to carry it off.'

'I'm not sure I have the nerve, though,' Andrea smiled. 'I—I'm used to more conservative colours and designs.'

'Which do nothing for your colouring or beauty,' came the retort. 'Come outside and see what Luke thinks.'

With an unusual sense of embarrassment, Andrea was intensely aware of Luke's glittering grey eyes ranging over her body. A shiver ran down her spine, almost as if he had physically touched her.

'Fantastic,' he said softly. 'I thought it might need some jewellery, but your looks are dazzling enough.' He glanced at Gillian, who was staring at Andrea with an expression of disbelief. 'What do you think?'

'I agree,' she answered shortly. 'Though she doesn't look like my Annie!'

'She's nobody's Annie any more. She's the great Andrea Markham. We'll take it,' he said. 'Now try on the next one.'

Feeling like a clothes horse, Andrea modelled a tangerine, paper taffeta ball gown that could have stepped out of a Gainsborough painting, had it not been for the wide green and gold jewelled belt that spanned her waist, and followed this with a stark black silk sheath that covered her from top to toe, yet by a miracle of seaming managed to indicate the perfect lines of her body.

'*That* is really sensational!' Gillian exclaimed. 'If you don't like it, Annie, I'll have it.'

'Andrea *is* having it, but it's not your style anyway,' Luke countered. 'Choose a couple of others, and I'll pay for them.'

'Oh, Luke, how sweet of you!'

'But unnecessary,' Andrea interposed, longing to shake her sister. 'I promised Gillian I'd treat her to something.'

'Allow me—for old times' sake,' he insisted with a winning smile, though it didn't win Andrea over, and she marched angrily into the fitting-room to change.

His extravagant gesture would encourage Gillian to believe he was still in love with her. And if he was, why had he flirted with herself last night? The sound of her sister's laughter and his deeper response sent a wave of jealousy spiralling through her that took her utterly by surprise. Yet why should it? He had all the attributes to turn a woman's head: looks, charm, intelligence, and an overpowering sensuality. Yet to contemplate an affair with him was dangerous, for she could easily lose her heart. Unless he fell in love with *her*. She almost laughed aloud. Luke wasn't the type to be happy with one woman. She had learned that as a child, and nothing she had read about him since had given her cause to change her opinion.

'Want any help with the zip?'

With a gasp she whirled round to see Luke standing behind her.

'It's usual to knock on a lady's door before you enter,' she snapped.

'We're such old friends, I didn't think you'd mind.'

'Well, I do. And on your way out, please ask a *vendeuse* to come in and help me.'

'You may have to wait a few minutes—they're all busy.' His eyes lowered to her back. 'There's a thread caught. If you'd let me release it...' Not waiting for permission, he reached out to do so, and she pulled away from him as if she'd been stung.

'Leave me be!' she cried.

Their eyes met in the mirror; hers dark indigo with anger, his silvery bright with curiosity. 'What are you frightened of?' he asked softly. 'You act like a woman who's never been touched by a man.'

'Spare me your amateur psychology,' she flared. 'I just object to being mauled.'

'Freeing your zip is mauling?' His lips curved mockingly. 'I'm beginning to think the gossip about you is true. *Have* you ever had a love-affair?'

'That's *my* affair. You manage my professional life, Luke, not my personal one.'

'Perhaps I'd like to manage both,' he challenged.

There was no mistaking the languorous glow in his eyes, and though she tried to remain aloof from it, her pulses quickened. 'Don't play games with me, Luke. I'm not one of your bimbos.'

'I wasn't treating you like one, nor am I playing games.'

His hands snaked out and encircled her waist, spinning her round to face him. She strained back, trying to pull free, but he lowered his dark head and captured her mouth. Logic told her to fight him but desire won and, like a sand-castle in the rain, her resistance crumbled. Relaxing in his hold, she enjoyed the feel of his hard, muscular body pressing against the softness of hers. As a teenager she had guiltily imagined such a moment, but never in her wildest dreams had she envisaged the sense of security, almost of homecoming, that his touch would engender.

His kiss was tender at first, but when she made no attempt to draw away it grew fiercer, and he parted her lips with his tongue, mating hers with his: hot, moist, soft, and tasting faintly of peppermint and another headily erotic flavour, uniquely his own.

His hands roamed in restless exploration over her satin-smooth shoulders, then down the length of her spine to her slender hips, pressing them against the flat tautness of his stomach. Andrea cradled his head, caressing the silky black hair and urging their kiss into a deeper intimacy. Their mouths became wild with longing: lips wet, engorged, marauding tongues sensuously entwined in an urgent duet of desire.

'Andrea,' he whispered upon her mouth, 'I want you...so much... But not here.' He dragged his lips away and ran them over her face, tracing the high cheekbones and nuzzling her ear, his breath warm, and insidiously arousing. 'Have dinner with me tonight. I want to romance you by candle-light, woo you with champagne, devour you in bed.'

Desire trembled her limbs, and the heat of it pulsed between her legs, making her intensely aware of every part of him: the slight roughness of dark stubble on his face, infinitely masculine and masterful; the strongly muscled arms; the hard wall of his chest and the throbbing swell of his arousal between the powerful columns of his thighs. Her entire being was pulsatingly alive, and she revelled in the magnitude of her response. She *wasn't* frigid; at last she had confirmation of it. Her affair with Roger had been lukewarm because it had mirrored her feelings for him. But with Luke she had experienced an all-consuming hunger that she had longed to appease, a passion so strong that she had wanted to be the taker as well as the giver.

Yet she dared not give, dared not take, for once she had opened herself to him she would be lost forever.

'No!' she cried aloud, and tore herself from his arms. 'I won't! I can't!'

Startled, he stared at her. 'Why not? You want me as much as I want you.'

'Don't read more into it than was there.' The effort of hiding her feelings robbed her voice of colour, and it came out flat and cold. 'You're an attractive devil and you caught me at a vulnerable moment.'

'I had the impression it was more than that.'

'It wasn't,' she said indifferently.

'Pity. We'd be good together.'

His comment—implying sexual coupling, nothing more—cut deep, but served to show how right she had been to reject him. 'My loss will be someone else's gain,' she said lightly, and could have cried with relief as Gillian rushed in.

'What do you think of this, Luke?' she asked, twirling round in a flurry of lilac chiffon.

'You look perfect,' he answered with such warmth that no one would have guessed that seconds before he had been making passionate love to another woman. 'Have you found anything else?'

'Yes. Come and see.'

They went out, and with a sigh Andrea sank on to a chair, exhausted by the emotions warring inside her. That Luke desired her came as no surprise. To him, every attractive woman was a challenge, and her coldness towards him had probably acted as a spur to the chase. But if so, why was he encouraging Gillian? Or was it a deliberate plan to lead her on and then hurt her by having an affair with her stepsister? The idea was machiavellian and she dismissed it. Luke might be manipulative but he wouldn't be so cruel.

The entry of a *vendeuse* forced Andrea to put Luke from her mind, and she made polite conversation as she was helped out of her dress.

'You look wonderful in dramatic clothes, Miss Markham,' the woman said. 'I'd love to show our entire collection.'

Andrea's reply was non-committal, though as she changed back into her suit she couldn't help acknowledging that the beige silk did little for her unusual colouring, and nothing whatever for her indigo-blue eyes.

Returning to the salon, she saw Gillian holding an emerald wool suit against herself.

'I love this one as well,' she was saying.

'Then try it on,' Luke suggested.

'But I have more need of two evening dresses.'

'You can have those as well.'

'Oh, Luke!' With an excited cry Gillian disappeared into a fitting-room.

'It isn't necessary for you to buy my sister any clothes,' Andrea said. 'I've already told her *I* would.'

'I made the offer to show I don't bear her any malice because of the past.'

'How generous of you,' Andrea said coldly.

'It has nothing to do with generosity. I did it because of you. Gillian's all the family you have and I wanted to be friends with her because of it.'

'I see.'

'Do you?' A shadow flickered across his face. 'I can't fathom why you have such a low opinion of me. Apart from venting my temper on you when you told me she'd gone off with another man, I don't know what I've done to deserve it.'

Because you're a womaniser, Andrea longed to say. Because you played around when you were engaged to Gillian, and because I'm still not sure what game you're playing with her now, nor what game you're playing with *me*. Yet she couldn't say any of this without giving away her feelings for him, and silently she wandered over to the window.

'Have dinner with me tonight and let's talk it out,' he went on, moving close to her.

'I can't. I'm tied up for the rest of the week.' She forced herself to meet his eyes. 'I've a recording session next Monday and I have to prepare for it.'

'Damn! I'd forgotten that. I'm not sure I'll be in the country.'

'It doesn't matter. You don't have to be there.'

'I'd like to be, though. If——'

'Luke, I need your help.' It was Gillian, rushing across to him with the emerald suit over one arm and a blue one over the other. 'I can't decide which colour I like best, so be a darling and choose one for me.'

'Take them both.'

'Both? You mean it? Oh, how wonderful!'

She rushed off, and Andrea, dismayed by her stepsister's avarice, said abruptly, 'I want those two suits put on *my* bill.'

'No.'

Luke's decisive retort brooked no argument, and Andrea was once again positive he was having an affair with her, regardless of what he had said. The knowledge was doubly painful: for herself, and for the misery that lay ahead of Gillian when he inevitably left her for someone else.

It was with a feeling of relief that she finally left the salon, intent on putting as much distance as possible between herself and Luke. But Gillian had other plans and, clinging to his arm, declared she was dying for a cup of tea and could they go to the Berkeley Hotel, which was round the corner?

Luke hesitated, then nodded. 'We'll have to make it a quick cup, I'm afraid. I have to get back to the office.'

'And I want to put in some practice, so I'll go home now,' Andrea added, signalling a passing cab and quickly stepping towards it.

But not quickly enough, for Luke was there with her, opening the door and favouring her with a piercing look.

'You won't always be able to run away from me,' he murmured, then in a louder voice said, 'I've made an appointment for you to see Gavin Dextor tomorrow at ten.' He named a Chelsea hairdresser who was currently the rave of the fashion magazines. 'There's no point wearing Hilary's clothes if the rest of you is dated.'

Before she could reply, he pressed some money into the cab driver's hand and stepped back.

Fuming, Andrea watched the tall, saturnine figure recede into the distance. No way was she going to have her hair restyled. If Luke didn't like it, he could lump it! How dared he act so presumptuously? If he behaved like this with his other artists, it was a wonder any of them stayed with him. If she didn't watch out, he would take over her entire life before she was aware of it.

She shivered at the thought. If only the tour were over and she could walk away from him. Until she did, she would live in fear.

CHAPTER SIX

IT WAS after six o'clock when Gillian came home and, to Andrea's relief, went straight upstairs. She knew that sooner or later she would hear about her tea at the Berkeley, though it looked as if she had a reprieve till dinner.

To her surprise Gillian only referred to it casually, remarking that the hotel didn't appear to have changed in the twelve years since she had been there.

'It was rude of you not to come with us,' she concluded. 'You can't still be holding a grudge against him because he was horrible to you when you were a kid!'

'Of course not.' Andrea gave a forced laugh. 'It's simply that I—I don't like his style of management.'

'I can't imagine why. He's a brilliant agent and impresario. Everyone says so. I wish you'd change your mind about him. I'd love the three of us to be close again, the way we used to be.' A dreamy expression softened the pert face. 'If I hadn't met Peter, Luke and I would be celebrating our twelfth wedding anniversary!'

Andrea's heart missed a beat. 'It's foolish thinking of might-have-beens.'

'How do you know it isn't a can-be? Luke's unmarried, and once I'm free . . .'

'You may feel differently then. You should date other men, give yourself a choice.'

'What choice have *you* ever given yourself? You're so single-minded about your career, you don't need anything or anyone else.'

'You're quite wrong,' Andrea retorted, irritated by the assumption. 'I just haven't met a man I'd fancy marrying.'

'I'm not surprised. If the way you behave with Luke is anything to go by, you'd scare away Dracula!'

'My relationship with Luke isn't a personal one; it's strictly business.'

'Then be businesslike,' Gillian stated. 'Luke can turn you into a superstar, and you'd earn a fortune.'

'I've more than enough money,' Andrea countered.

'All right. So if you don't want to be nice to him for your own sake, be nice to him for mine.'

'Luke's a big boy, Gillian. I'm sure my behaviour to him won't affect his attitude to *you*.'

'I know,' came the confident reply. 'But it would be less embarrassing for me if you weren't so snappy with him.'

'And less embarrassing for *me*,' Andrea rejoined, 'if you had the decency to tell him you aren't yet divorced.'

'I almost did this afternoon, but we were having such a marvellous time that I didn't want to rock the boat.' Gillian sipped her wine. 'I want more than an affair with him, you know.'

Andrea lowered her eyes, afraid her feelings might seep through them. She had often wondered whether Luke and Gillian had been lovers when they were engaged, but had never asked—perhaps because she hadn't really wanted to know.

'He was sensational in bed,' her stepsister continued. 'I think that's why I was never happy with Peter. I kept comparing them.'

So now I do know, Andrea thought, but aloud said, 'None of your letters ever hinted you were unhappy. You even wrote that you were planning a family.'

'No, I didn't,' came the sharp retort. 'You must have misunderstood. Peter was the one who wanted children, not me. I've no patience with them.'

'Since when? You always enjoyed being around children.'

'Well, I've changed. Now for heaven's sake stop going on about Peter and me.'

There was a hysterical edge to Gillian's voice, and Andrea instantly changed the subject. 'I believe there's a good film on TV. Finish your sweet and we'll go into the drawing-room and watch it.'

A short while later they were both relaxing in front of the screen. But Andrea's ease was a pretence, for she was worried by her stepsister's mood swings. Yet she could not force a confidence from someone who was unwilling to give it; all she could do was sit back and wait.

Next morning she decided to keep the hairdressing appointment Luke had made for her. She was tied to him for the moment and it was foolish to keep fighting him. Besides, if she went on doing it he might think she was acting out of pique because he was friendly towards Gillian! The notion was enough to send her scurrying to Chelsea.

The white and gold salon was bustling when she arrived, and several clients had faces familiar from magazines and television. As soon as she had given her name, Gavin Dextor came over to welcome her. He was small and thin, with a boyish smile and a crew cut, and couldn't have been more than in his mid-twenties.

'I'm a great fan of yours,' he said as he showed her to a black leather armchair. 'I have every one of your recordings, and I tape you whenever you play on television.'

Andrea smiled but did not believe a word of it; it was the sort of thing many people said when meeting her for the first time. But as Gavin went on talking he displayed such knowledge of her performances that she realised she had done him an injustice, and her misgivings at being here lessened. Such a devoted fan surely wouldn't scalp her with his scissors, as so many hairdressers had tried to do!

'You have such wonderful hair,' he murmured as he took out the confining pins and the silken mass fell around her shoulders. 'It's criminal not to let the texture and colour be seen.'

'I can't have it falling round my face,' she said firmly.

'I understand. But if you'd allow me to restyle it, I——'

'That's why Miss Markham is here,' a voice, instantly recognisable as Luke's, cut in from behind her. 'As long as you keep it soft yet sophisticated, you can do what you like.'

Gavin chuckled, and Andrea glared at Luke in the mirror, a warm flush staining her skin as he scrutinised her long, silky tresses, the colour of newly polished ebony. Remembering her decision to be more amenable towards him, she forced a smile to her lips.

'I didn't expect to see you here, Luke.'

'How could Pygmalion not see his Galatea?' he said smoothly, before directing his gaze to the hairdresser. 'How long will it take?'

'Two hours.'

'I'll be back,' he stated. 'Make sure Miss Markham has some lunch—she has a busy afternoon ahead of her and I don't want her wilting through lack of food!'

'There's no——' Andrea began, then stopped as she realised she was talking to Luke's departing figure. He really was the most infuriating, domineering, conceited... Fuming, she ran out of appropriate adjectives, then, recognising the futility of the exercise, gave herself up to Gavin's capable hands.

She kept her eyes averted from the mirror for the entire proceedings, and it was not until he had reached the final stage that she allowed herself to see what he had done.

The change was so startling, she barely recognised herself. Her hair was a mass of soft waves, falling in raven richness to her slender shoulders. Used to wearing it pulled back into a tight knot, she was conscious of the weight against her face, and put up her hands to push it away.

'Don't,' Luke instructed, coming up behind her. 'You'll ruin the effect.' He smiled at Gavin. 'You've performed another miracle.'

The younger man grinned. 'With a client who looks like Miss Markham, it's no miracle.'

'True,' Luke agreed as he settled the bill, and said no more until they were outside. 'I've fixed you a photographic session with Jack Lenton. We must hurry. We're already late.'

'The only place I'm going is home,' Andrea said quietly. 'In future please consult me before you make any appointments. I'm an established artist, not a newcomer you're trying to promote, and I won't be treated as such.'

'Then stop fighting me,' Luke said. 'Your contract gives me the right to promote you as I see fit, so I suggest you resign yourself to the inevitable.'

'And if I don't?'

'I'll sue you for breach of contract.'

'You wouldn't.'

'Try me.'

She stopped dead and faced him. Black denim jeans and shirt emphasised his tanned skin, turning his silver-grey eyes to ice. His expression was grim, and his motionless stance, coupled with his colouring, put her in mind of a Red Indian warrior sizing up his enemy. And he *was* the enemy. She mustn't forget it.

'Don't fight me, Andrea,' he warned softly.

'I would if it were just me. But I don't want to ruin Bella.'

'Keep remembering that.'

'All I want to remember is that once the tour's over, I'll be free of you!'

She resumed walking and he guided her to the car park, where he had left his car.

'The studio's in Docklands,' he said as they emerged into the daylight.

'It will take us ages to get there,' she muttered. 'Doesn't the waste of time irritate you?'

'We have no choice. It's where he works.'

'But your time is worth money,' she persisted.

'Money isn't my main motivation. Not any more. I'm in this business because I love it. Though I have to confess I derive great satisfaction from knowing I've managed to earn the respect of my peers without forsaking my principles.'

'Don't you think selling your artists like cans of beans in a supermarket *is* forsaking them?'

'Not at all. I'm not damaging the quality of the product—merely altering the packaging.'

'Talking of packaging, I don't have a change of clothes,' she said with satisfaction. 'And all photographers insist on that.'

'Not to worry,' Luke grinned. 'I asked Hilary to send round a selection.'

Defeated, Andrea slumped in the seat and stared out of the window.

Jack Lenton's studio was in a converted warehouse overlooking the Thames, and the light flooding in through the wall-to-wall glass windows was so dazzling that she wondered at the need for extra lighting. As she had come to expect from the people with whom Luke worked, the photographer was no older than herself, while his three assistants were almost teenagers.

For the next few hours she changed into half a dozen different outfits and posed and postured as ordered. Reggae music blared from quadraphonic speakers, and though it wasn't something she normally enjoyed, she found herself reacting to the strong sensual beat. Unlike his behaviour at the couturier's, Luke gave no orders or comments, but sat on a chair in the far corner, making calls on his mobile telephone. Yet she was positive he had told Jack Lenton the image he wanted him to create.

'You're a natural, darling,' the photographer encouraged, clicking away at the camera without cessation.

He was known for the naturalness and vivacity of his pictures, and to achieve this he took dozens at the same setting, though from different angles, talking to her all the while, and making her laugh at many of his anecdotes.

'Don't lift the neckline,' he ordered as she tried to adjust the top of a tight-fitting black velvet dress. 'You've got great boobs, so don't hide 'em.'

'I'm not a *Playboy* centre-fold!' she retorted. 'And you're giving a completely false impression of me.'

'I want to show the public how gorgeous you are. But if you want to give them a false image, OK.'

'It's not a false image. I never wear such low-cut necklines.'

'It isn't low. You're just a prude.'

Her eyes flashed fire and he laughed and went on snapping. 'Great! Great! Now you're really alive.'

'Why do I get the feeling I'm being manipulated?' she asked, unable to prevent a smile.

'Because you are!' he grinned, and clicked some more.

When another two rolls of film had been exhausted he signalled that he had finished, and Andrea, surprisingly, found herself apologising for her earlier bad temper.

'I've been a bit of a pill, haven't I?'

'Only for the first hour!'

'I didn't want an honest reply!'

'Yes, you did. You're an honest woman. When I look at someone in my lens, I see their character as well as their body.'

Andrea turned away. Until Luke had come into her life again, she would have agreed with the photographer's assessment. But in the past four days she had run from honesty and lived a lie. And if Gillian and Luke did eventually marry, she'd have to go on doing it.

Keeping her face expressionless, she walked across to him. He was deep in conversation, the small mobile phone cradled in one long-fingered hand, and she had an opportunity of studying him; not that she needed to, for his image was imprinted on her mind's eye: the high cheekbones, the tanned skin stretched tightly over them, the short thick lashes fringing his eyes, the silky black hair worn in a style more suitable to a rock singer than an entrepreneur of classical music. Yet it suited him. She couldn't deny it. Seen from the front, his hair looked as if it were cut short and sculpted close to his skull. But from the side the short pony-tail was visible, held in place by a narrow black crocodile band. How did he look with his hair loose? she mused, and instantly had a picture of a handsome Cavalier with jet-black locks and mocking eyes.

As she reached him he ended his conversation and rose. 'You must be tired from being under the lights,' he said. 'Thank you for being so co-operative with Jack.'

'I had no choice!'

'True. But you obeyed your dictator with great charm.'

'I don't quite see you as a dictator,' she said, deliberately misinterpreting his comment, and had the pleasure of seeing him look disconcerted.

But he was soon in control of himself, and as they drove away from Docklands their talk veered on the inconsequential rather than the personal, as if neither wished to quarrel.

'As a matter of interest,' she said, 'how many calls did you make this afternoon?'

'Four overseas, and lord knows how many local ones.'

'I'm surprised you don't have a fax in your car!'

'I have. In the back. And it's not a status symbol, if that's what you're going to say.'

'I wasn't. At the pace you work, it's a necessity.'

He slanted her a quick glance. 'That's the first time you've missed an opportunity to be sarcastic with me. I hope it augurs well for the future?'

She shrugged. 'I'm stuck with you for the next few months, and it's less wearing on my nerves to have a truce.'

'I'm glad to hear it. With any luck, you might even realise I'm not the devil incarnate.'

'Just a highly articulate man who knows what he wants.'

'And gets it!' he reminded her.

'By not wasting a single minute.' Cleverly she twisted his answer. 'I'm surprised you don't have a chauffeur too. Then you could work while you're travelling.'

'I do have a chauffeur, but he's doing some errands for me today. If you'd accepted my dinner invitation last night you'd have met Justin.'

'An unusual name for a driver,' she remarked.

'He's an unusual fellow. We were at school together and lost touch when he went into stockbroking. A couple of years ago the pressure got to him and he contacted me. Saw my advert for a chauffeur in the paper, and took the job temporarily—until he'd got himself together again. After six months he found he didn't want to return to the rat race.' Again Luke slanted her a glance. 'Like me, he knows money isn't everything.'

The car slowed as they approached the city, and Andrea became aware that he was heading towards north London. 'I live too far out for you to take me home,' she protested. 'I can easily pick up a taxi.'

'Don't be silly.'

'Please,' she insisted, and at her tone he drew into the kerb.

'Very well. I don't want to do anything to upset our truce! And now we've established it, perhaps you'll have dinner with me tonight?'

Andrea was tempted to accept, but the thought of Gillian made her shake her head. 'I'm sorry, but I can't. I've already lost half a day's practice, and with the recording on Monday ahead of me...'

'Another time perhaps.'

His voice was crisp and she sensed his annoyance, though he gave no sign of it as he hailed a taxi and saw her into it.

'I'll see you at the studio on Monday,' he said as he slipped the cabbie some money. 'Have a good week.'

Disappointment flooded her that he had not suggested another date, which was irrational of her, to say the least, for the problem of Gillian remained. As did her own feelings for him, for they warned her that getting involved with him would lead to pain.

Gillian was crossing the hall as she entered the house, and gave a cry of delight as she saw her.

'I adore your hair,' she exclaimed. 'It makes you look really sexy, instead of like a schoolmarm! Luke's words, not mine,' she confessed. 'But I'm sure he won't mind my quoting him.'

'When did you speak to him?' Andrea asked with surprise.

'He just telephoned.'

Andrea's pulse-rate quickened. Had he called to persuade her to change her mind? Maybe she'd go out with him after all.

'He's taking me out to dinner,' Gillian went on. 'You don't mind if I go, do you?'

'Of course not.' So much for thinking his invitation had meant something. He had merely had a free evening and had considered it diplomatic to try to cash in on her declared truce.

With leaden steps she went upstairs to change into her practice gear—a pure silk caftan, light and loose-fitting—then went into the drawing-room and sat at the piano. Music was her solace, her companion, and never let her down.

It was near midnight when she went to bed, relaxed and tired. She fell asleep at once but awoke with a start at two o'clock. Had Gillian called her? Yawning, she padded down the hall to listen at the bedroom door. There was no sound, yet she was still worried, and she carefully slipped the latch and peeped in. The room was empty, the bed not yet slept in.

Instantly she was wide awake, imagination running riot as she envisaged Gillian in Luke's arms. Not on the dance-floor at a nightclub, but in his bed.

As if demons were after her, she ran back to her room and slammed the door. She was hot, then cold, shivering as though with fever. But the fever was jealousy and there was no antibiotic one could take for it. It was an illness she alone could conquer. And she would.

CHAPTER SEVEN

ANDREA did not see Gillian until lunchtime next day when, her head still filled with the music she had been playing, she went into the dining-room and found her at the table.

'Don't you get bored, bashing away at the piano for hours on end?' her stepsister asked.

'A diplomat you're not!' Andrea smiled, amused at the less than complimentary way her playing had been described. '"Bashing away at the piano" gives me more pleasure than anything else I know.'

'At your age, you should be saying that about a man!'

'Perhaps I will, one day.' Andrea ate a piece of melon. 'And talking of men, how was your evening with Luke?'

'Sensational. He's the world's most wonderful dancer. I told him he should have been a promoter of pop music, not boring old classical stuff.'

'What did he say to that?'

'Said he's going to call me Phyllis.'

'Phyllis?'

'Short for philistine!' Gillian stifled a yawn. 'Gosh, I'm absolutely exhausted. I didn't get back till three.'

'Well, if you *will* dance till then ...'

'We weren't dancing. Luke invited me to his home and we talked for hours.'

Poised to hear more—Gillian was usually keen to expound on her dates with him—Andrea was surprised when she started talking about an old girlfriend she had contacted that morning.

'I told her you'll be practising like crazy for the next few days, and she asked me to spend the weekend with her in Brighton. Luke's gone to Sweden and won't be back till Monday, so I might as well go.'

Andrea hid her chagrin. Although she had told him it was unnecessary for him to be at the recording studio with her, he had categorically stated that he would be there. Yet the lure of Sweden—probably some blonde Swedish beauty, she surmised sourly—had proved a stronger enticement.

'I'm sorry I'm so busy,' she said aloud. 'But once the recording session is out of the way——'

'You'll be preparing for the tour and be busier than ever!' Gillian laughed. 'Don't worry about me, darling. I'm just happy being with you and Luke again.'

Especially Luke, Andrea thought, but knew better than to say so. Once again she wondered how Gillian's relationship with him would develop. Were his intentions 'honourable', as her stepsister assumed, or was she simply a new addition to his stable of lovelies?

It was a question that plagued her for the rest of the week, and though she managed to push it away during the long hours she spent at the piano, once the ivory keys were still, her mind was busy with it.

It was a relief to go to the studio in St John's Wood on Monday morning, and with a comforting feeling of familiarity, for she had been there often, she walked up the narrow path that led to what looked like a rambling old mansion. But inside it had been cleverly turned into a spacious, ultra-modern studio, big enough to house a full orchestra, though today there was only herself, for over the next two days she would be recording three Beethoven sonatas and five by Scarlatti.

Entering the sound-proof room, she glanced towards the glass partition behind which lay the vast bank of complex, highly expensive equipment that would faithfully record every note and nuance of her playing, and smiled at Tim Banks, the sound engineer who recorded all her records.

He grinned and waved, then glanced over his shoulder as a tall black-haired man came into the booth. Luke! Andrea's heart missed a beat. He was supposed to be in Sweden, yet here he was, staring at her with one dark eyebrow raised, as if he knew exactly how she felt.

Hastily she turned and went over to the piano, making a pretence of checking it, though she knew full well it was in perfect condition. Hugo Bethel, who supervised all her records, came in and greeted her warmly. He did not say how strange it was for them to be here without Abraham, but his extra-long handclasp spoke for him. Sudden tears drenched her eyes.

'We'll take a sound level,' he said. 'Then we'll be ready to go.'

For the next five hours, with a one-hour break for lunch, which she ate alone in a room reserved for her sole use—when recording she liked to eschew all conversation and company—Andrea gave life to the deeply felt emotion and violence that characterised the Beethoven sonatas she had chosen to play. Little had she known when she had decided on them months ago that they would so exactly mirror the emotions Luke aroused in her!

She was exhausted when she finally came to the end of the session, and she dropped her hands in her lap and glanced towards the sound recordist's booth, relieved when Tim gave her the thumbs-up sign.

Luke was no longer there and she was part relieved, part piqued that he had not remained until the end. But in this she had done him an injustice, for as Hugo walked with her to the entrance, he came out of one of the offices.

'You did an excellent job, Hugo,' he said. 'But then you always do.' Dark eyes focused on Andrea. 'It was a joy listening to you. If tomorrow goes as well, you'll have every reason to be delighted.'

'Thank you, Luke.'

'Do you have your car, or may I drive you home?'

'I have my car, thanks.'

'I'll see you to it.'

She nodded, wondering why he had to look so devastating. A silver-grey silk T-shirt clung to his chest, the muscles rippling clearly beneath the fabric. The colour echoed his eyes and emphasised his dark attraction and strong angular features. He smelt faintly of Aramis, though beneath it was the more intimate scent of the man himself: warm and earthy and immensely appealing.

'I didn't expect to see you,' she commented. 'Gillian said you'd be in Sweden until today.'

'I was.'

'But you were in the studio at nine!'

'I chartered a plane.'

Andrea gaped at him, and aware of her astonishment, he wagged a finger at her.

'I told you I'd be here and I always try to keep my word.'

For an instant she couldn't help being flattered, then chided herself for her naïveté. He was simply pulling out all the stops to show her what a caring manager he was; and since he would be richer by many thousands of pounds if she remained with him, it wasn't surprising he was going to such trouble.

'I shan't chance my luck and ask you to have dinner with me this evening,' he murmured as they reached her car and he took the key from her hand to open the door. 'I'm sure you'll be busy practising.'

She nodded and slipped into the driving seat. 'Why not try Gillian if you're at a loose end? If she's free, she'll be delighted to accept.'

'I'm still recovering from our last date,' he said smoothly. 'She kept me up till all hours.'

His reply was annoyingly ambiguous—a trait he had mastered—and she ignored it.

'I'll see you tomorrow,' she said, and before he could answer, switched on the engine and drove off.

As Luke's figure diminished, her anger—directed at herself—increased. By speaking to him the way she had, she had again given him reason to believe she was jealous. So much for her intention of trying to be calm and friendly towards him!

By the time she reached home, Luke had telephoned and invited Gillian to dinner, and she was bubbling with high spirits. The weekend with her friend had gone well, and she appeared rested and less brittle. The sun had flecked her gold hair with silver and given colour to her pale skin, though the shadows beneath her brown eyes remained.

'How did things go at the studio?' she enquired, almost as an afterthought.

'Very well. I——' But Andrea was talking to herself, for Gillian was already halfway up the stairs, intent on getting ready.

In a mood as blue as the Wedgwood bowl on the hall table, Andrea went in to the music-room, seeking solace in the only way she knew.

She was at the piano when she heard Luke arrive, and drowned Gillian's cry of welcome with a robust burst of chords, which she maintained until she heard the throaty growl of his departing car. But no sooner had it gone when there was a knock at the door. Knowing that Mrs Prentice knew better than to disturb her unless it was urgent, she looked round in alarm.

'What is it?'

'There's a gentleman on the telephone asking for Mrs Maynard.'

'Didn't you tell him she was out?'

'Of course. But the reason I came in was because he asked to speak to you instead, and became extremely angry when I told him you were busy.'

With a premonition of trouble ahead, Andrea went into the hall and lifted the receiver. 'Miss Markham speaking,' she said.

'Hello, Annie,' the man replied. 'This is Peter.'

'I'm called Andrea now,' she corrected automatically. 'How are you?'

'Fine. Where's Gillian?'

'She's visiting friends,' Andrea swiftly improvised.

'What time do you expect her back?'

Andrea hesitated a moment. 'She doesn't want to talk to you.'

'That doesn't surprise me. But *I* want to talk to *her*. I'm staying at the Wainright Hotel and I'll be with you in half an hour.'

'She won't be back until late tonight.'

'I don't believe you.' His tone was harsh.

'I promise you, it's true. Look, Peter, Gillian isn't well and seeing you might upset her.'

'Not well?' There was an instant's silence. 'She hasn't done anything foolish again, has she?'

'What do you mean?'

'Don't you know? She ... well, she ...'

'You mean she attempted suicide?' Andrea guessed.

'Yes,' Peter said heavily. 'After that I kept all her drugs locked away. For God's sake, do the same!'

'I have. All she's taking now are the ones prescribed by my doctor.'

Peter's sigh of relief was audible. 'It seems you've grown into a sensible young woman.'

'We all grow and change,' she replied pointedly.

He picked up her implication. 'Has Gillian told you I've turned into some sort of a monster?' he questioned.

'According to her, you're hardly the perfect husband,' Andrea responded guardedly.

'*That*,' he retorted quickly, 'is part of her illness.'

'Do you honestly think it will *help* to see her? She's set on a divorce.'

'I'll fight it! For pity's sake, Andrea, I *love* her.'

His distress sounded so genuine that Andrea's antagonism towards him started to dissolve.

'I don't know your side of the story,' she averred slowly. 'But my main concern right now is Gillian's health. Seeing you is bound to upset her.'

'She has to face me sooner or later. I'm as distraught as she is about the accident and the baby.'

'Accident? Baby?' Andrea was aghast.

'You mean she hasn't told you?' The anger drained from his voice and he sounded weary. 'She'd started labour, and we were on our way to the hospital when we had a crash. Gillian wasn't badly hurt but the child was stillborn.'

'I didn't even know she was pregnant! Why didn't she tell me?'

'She'd had several miscarriages and she didn't want anyone to know till the baby was born.'

Andrea swallowed hard. 'But why has she turned against you? Was the accident your fault?'

'No. Some maniac came out of a side-road and smashed right into us. The poor devil was killed but the court gave me an absolute acquittal. Unfortunately, Gillian wouldn't accept the verdict. The doctor said she needed to blame *someone* for the loss of the baby and I was the obvious choice.'

Andrea sank on to a chair. 'I'm so sorry! How awful for you.'

'Yes, it was—it *is*. Look, can we meet somewhere to talk?'

'Not tonight, I'm afraid. But I can make it tomorrow, as long as it's near the studio where I'm working.'

'Where's that?'

'St John's Wood. I can meet you outside the Underground at one o'clock.'

'Fine.' His tone was happier. 'Give Gillian my love and——'

'I don't think that's a good idea at this stage,' Andrea cut in. 'I'll see you tomorrow.'

Replacing the receiver, she noticed her hands were trembling. She had not yet taken in what Peter had told her but she didn't doubt his veracity. How dreadful it all was! Gillian had not only lost a child, but blamed and hated her husband for it. Furthermore she had attempted to kill herself. It was this that frightened Andrea the most.

CHAPTER EIGHT

THE following morning Andrea was overcome by guilt at the prospect of seeing Peter behind Gillian's back. Yet she knew that in her stepsister's present state of mind it was unwise to let her know he was in England.

She was thinking about it when she entered the studio in St John's Wood, but sight of Luke in the sound recordist's booth brought her own emotional problems to the fore. He acknowledged her arrival with a brief raise of his hand, though she noticed that his eyes lingered on her for quite a while before he resumed speaking to the man next to him.

Self-consciously she turned away, smoothing her hair. She had taken pains to choose an outfit that complemented it: a Hilary Dix suit in cream linen that Luke had chosen for her. Its short-sleeved single-breasted jacket hugged her waist, and the knee-skimming A-line skirt showed off her long, shapely legs.

'Ready to take a sound level?' Hugo Bethel asked, coming towards her, and she nodded, her professionalism asserting itself as she concentrated on the session ahead.

Today she was playing Scarlatti, and because the sonatas she had chosen were all one-movement ones, any error she made meant her going back to the beginning.

It was a relief when they broke for lunch, and her spirits rose higher when she saw Luke striding into the studio, his fist raised triumphantly, his face alight.

'Terrific!' he raved. 'We have perfect takes of the three sonatas, so you've only two more to do.'

Happily she smiled and flexed her fingers. 'Once this recording's over, I think I'll give Scarlatti a miss!'

'Your public may not let you. When they hear this album I think you'll be regarded as his greatest exponent.' Silver-grey eyes crinkled at the corners as he surveyed her. 'I hope you'll agree that I know what suits you!'

'Even if I didn't, I wouldn't waste my time saying so. You always do what you want, anyway.'

Before he had a chance to answer, Hugo joined them, and she watched Luke's face animate as he talked to the other man. Only as he turned his head did she notice that his hair had been cut, and instead of the ponytail, his thick dark mane now stopped just short of his white silk polo sweater. It made him look younger, and she couldn't restrain the spasm of sexual awareness that swept over her as he swung round to her again and she took in the hard, tanned leanness of his face and the full curve of his half-smiling lips.

'As we don't have so much to record,' he said, 'I've suggested we take a two-hour break. I know a nice restaurant where we——'

'Sorry, but I'm meeting someone for lunch,' she replied truthfully.

His expression showed his disbelief, but there was no way she could explain, and silently she watched him give her a brief nod and walk away.

Andrea left the studio and headed towards her arranged rendezvous with Peter. Would she recognise him? After all, it was twelve years since they had met. But she knew his lanky frame instantly, though his fair hair had a touch of silver, and worry lines were etched on his forehead and either side of his mouth.

'Annie!' Catching her hands, he kissed her cheek. 'I must say the photographs you sent Gillian don't do you justice. You look fabulous.'

'You don't look so bad yourself,' she lied.

'That might have been true six months ago but not now. I've been worried sick about Gilly. Is——?'

'There's a restaurant near by we can go to,' Andrea cut in. 'It's better if we talk there.'

Taking the hint, he chatted about life 'down under' until they were seated at a window-table in an Italian restaurant in St John's Wood High Street. Only then did he refer to his wife.

'How is she? Still depressed and sleeping badly?'

'Not any more. But she tends to be rather excitable. She doesn't know you're in London, of course.'

'I think she should. She's my wife and I want to see her.' He leaned forward, his grey eyes bewildered. 'I don't know what she told you about our marriage, but I give you my word everything was great till we lost the baby. That's when she went to pieces.'

'According to Gillian, you neglected her. She——' Andrea stopped as their first course—gnocchi with cream and tomato coulis—was set before them, and did not speak until the waiter had gone. 'She said you left her alone a great deal.'

'That was mainly her doing. I was building up my business and she accepted that I had to work all hours. To begin with she helped me, but once we were in the money, she chose to stay home and seemed happy pottering in the house.'

'So everything was fine until the accident?'

'Yes. Afterwards she refused to see me for weeks, and when she finally did, she accused me of trying to kill her and the baby!'

Andrea was startled. 'I'm sure she didn't mean it—not deep down.'

'That's what the psychiatrist who was looking after her said. And he seemed to be right, for several weeks later she seemed normal—apart from being depressed—and she came home.'

'If you'd let me know about the accident I'd have flown out to see her.'

'She wouldn't let me tell you. She had this crazy notion that if anyone else knew she'd lost the baby, she'd never be able to have another! After a few weeks at home she was like her old self, and I started going to the office. Then one afternoon I came back and found she'd gone. It didn't take me long to discover she was with you, and as soon as I'd arranged for someone to run my business, I came here to bring her home.'

'She won't go with you,' Andrea said quietly. 'And my doctor—who's looking after her—warned me not to put any pressure on her. I'm sure her psychiatrist told you the same.'

After a momentary hesitation, Peter nodded, his whole demeanour one of dejection. 'Did she actually say she wants a divorce?'

'Yes.'

'To marry Luke Kane?'

Andrea was astonished. 'How did you guess?'

'She talked about him non-stop after the accident. Kept saying she felt guilty for the way she had treated him, and that losing the baby was her punishment.'

'What rubbish!' Andrea shook her head. 'I'll have a word with Dr Marshall when I get home and see what he suggests. I hope you'll take his advice, Peter. He's an excellent doctor.'

Andrea was still mulling over Gillian's behaviour when she returned to the studio, and to release her tension she went straight to the piano. She was soothing herself with the 'Moonlight' Sonata when a sixth sense told her that Luke had entered the recording booth, and it was an effort not to look round at him.

The afternoon session went as well as the first, and at six o'clock Hugo declared himself satisfied.

'We'll have a finished play-back for you to hear at the end of next week. Is ten o'clock Friday all right for you?'

'That's fine.' She rose and stretched. 'When I hear it I'll probably want to redo the whole thing! I always feel I can do better.'

'I doubt if you'll do better than yesterday or today,' Luke affirmed, appearing beside her.

She half turned to him but avoided meeting his eyes. 'I can see why you're such a popular manager. You know how to massage one's ego!'

'I'd never lie to an artist about their performance.'

'Have you ever lost one by telling them an unpalatable truth?'

'Two,' he admitted, smiling. 'One retired six months later, and the other went to another agent and then begged me to take him back!'

'Did you?'

'Naturally. Since he was intelligent enough to admit he was wrong, I was intelligent enough not to say "I told you so"!'

Against her will, Andrea laughed, and as if taking advantage of her relaxed mood, Luke put his hand under her elbow.

'I didn't see your car parked in the street, so I'll drive you home,' he said, his tone brooking no argument.

Accepting his offer with a casual acquiescence she did not feel, she went with him to his car. Belting herself into the passenger-seat, she was absurdly nervous, for the strength of his presence was almost tangible. As the car moved slowly forward, hemmed in by the rush-hour traffic, she glanced at him. His body was relaxed yet there was a frown on his face, and she wondered what was troubling him.

'Who was the man you were lunching with?' he asked suddenly, staring straight ahead.

'Do you own a spy satellite?' she retorted.

'I was driving down the high street on my way to town and saw you going into a restaurant.'

'You should have joined us,' she said sweetly. 'The food's excellent there.'

'You haven't answered my question.'

'Why should I? It's no business of yours.'

'What's the big secret—or is he married?' Luke glanced at her and, seeing her redden, put two and two together and made five. 'So that's it,' he said tersely. 'You disappoint me.'

Wishing she could be honest, but afraid that if she was he might tell Gillian, she was forced to be defensive. 'You are the last person who should proffer lessons in morals, Luke.'

His lips tightened. '*I've* always made it a rule never to get involved with anyone who was married.'

'What category does Gillian fall into, then?'

'As her divorce is nearly through, I'd say single.'

Andrea clamped her mouth shut, hard put to it not to tell him the truth. Only the knowledge of Gillian's precarious mental state kept her silent.

'Why do we always end up talking about Gillian?' he demanded irritably. 'She's a grown woman and can take care of herself.'

'She happens to be very highly strung at the moment.'

'She'll be fine once she's free. But enough about Gillian. It's you I want to talk about.' The car stopped at a red light and he took the opportunity of staring at her directly. 'I still can't get over not recognising you from the photographs on your record albums. But you're nothing like the kid I remembered—except for your eyes. They're still like smoky amethysts.'

Warmth enveloped her and she was dismayed he could make her feel so gauche; almost like the teenager she had once been, whom he was now remembering.

'I'll never forget when you walked into my office last month,' he went on. 'I thought you were a stranger yet I felt as if you'd always been a part of my life.'

'Perhaps it was because you enjoyed my records.'

'Perhaps.' He hesitated, then said abruptly, 'How long does Gillian intend staying with you?'

Andrea's pleasure evaporated. And he had the nerve to accuse *her* of continually talking about her stepsister!

'I'm not sure,' she replied stiffly. 'We haven't discussed it.'

'Wouldn't it be better for you if she had her own place?'

'Does her living in my home curb your style?'

'Yes,' he said bluntly, accelerating as the lights turned to green.

Andrea trembled with fury. No one could accuse him
of mincing his words. Yet the fact that he hadn't was
reassuring, showing that he had no idea he had turned
her personal world topsy-turvy.

'No comment, Andrea?'

'None.'

'Still defensive with me?'

'Let's say I'm on my guard.'

His sigh was audible. 'I wish you'd relax and trust
me. I have your best interests at heart.'

Musically, there was no doubt he did, but on the personal level she would have no peace until he was out of
her life. Her mind boggled at the thought of his having
an ongoing relationship with Gillian, and she determined to do all she could for Peter.

Luke slowed the car as they approached the narrow
hill leading to her home. 'Have dinner with me tonight. On a strictly platonic basis, of course,' he added
drily. 'You're as taut as a drum and it will do you good
to relax.'

She longed to say yes but wouldn't give herself the
pleasure. How could she when he had only asked her
out because she was a client he was anxious to soothe?

'I can't,' she said flatly.

'Can't or won't?'

'I've another engagement.'

'The man you lunched with today?'

She did not answer, and neither of them spoke until
he drew up in front of her house.

'Care to come in for a drink?' she offered, knowing
she should proffer an olive branch.

'Why not?' he replied offhandedly, and followed her
inside.

The sound of their voices brought Gillian out of the drawing-room. She looked rested and pretty, and Luke bent and kissed her lightly on the cheek.

'A lazy life suits you,' he teased.

'I've been thinking it's time I took a job.' She linked her arm through his. 'Maybe *you* have one for me?'

'Even if I did, I wouldn't recommend it. I'm an extremely tough boss!'

Gillian pouted and he knuckled her cheek, causing Andrea to suppress a strong urge to kick him. How dared he stand there and flirt with Gillian in this idiotic manner? Particularly when only a few moments ago he had invited *her* out to dinner? Except that his invitation had been prompted by professional interest, and she would do well to remember it.

'Give Luke a drink, Gillian,' she said quietly. 'I'll join you later. I have to call someone first.'

Hurrying upstairs to her room, she dialled Dr Marshall's number. Luckily he was in, and she told him of her meeting with Peter.

'It explains a great deal,' the doctor commented, 'and answers most of the questions that have been puzzling me. Your sister's improving, as I'm sure you've seen, but it would be better if she herself told you about the accident and the baby, rather than have her forced into it because of her husband's arrival here.'

'So you don't think I should tell her he's in London?'

'Right. I think she needs more time to come to terms with the trauma of the accident. When she has, she'll be better able to sort things out with him.'

'I hope it won't be too late by then. Luke Kane, my temporary manager, was engaged to her years ago, and since they've met again she imagines herself in love with him.'

'That's a problem,' Dr Marshall agreed. 'But I stand by what I said.'

Reluctantly Andrea relayed these comments to Peter, relieved when he accepted the doctor's advice, albeit unhappily.

'How long did he say I must wait?' he asked.

'He wasn't specific. I suppose it depends how quickly Gillian recovers.'

'If she's well enough to be going out with Luke and thinking of a divorce——'

'That doesn't mean she's well,' Andrea interrupted. 'It could mean the opposite! Maybe you should return to Australia and I'll let you know when to come back.'

'I'm not leaving without her,' came the stubborn retort. 'I can do some business on the Continent, so I'll go to Holland and Germany for a few weeks. I'll let you have my itinerary as soon as I've worked it out.'

'Do that,' she said, relieved that he would be occupied and therefore less likely to worry. 'It will be better if you don't call me here in case——'

'I get the picture,' he said bitterly. 'I'll post it to you in a typewritten envelope marked private.'

Appreciating his hurt, Andrea returned to the drawing-room and found Luke alone.

'Gillian's changing,' he explained. 'We're going out to dinner.'

'How nice!' Andrea smiled through gritted teeth. 'I'll be able to have an early night.'

'I thought you had another engagement?' he came back at her fast.

'I *did* have,' she lied. 'But I'm tired and cancelled it. That's the call I just made.'

'I don't believe you had a date.' He came closer to her. 'What's with you, Andrea? I thought you'd put your prejudices against me aside?'

'I have.'

'Professionally perhaps. But on a personal level you hate my guts!'

Aware of his surveyal, every part of her came pulsatingly alive. Was she simply prey to sexual attraction or did it go deeper? Frightened to search for the answer, she banished the question.

'You're reading too much into my behaviour, Luke. It's just unfortunate I've been busy every time you asked me out.'

'Then give me a date when you're free,' he said at once, 'and I'll make myself available.'

She was searching for an excuse when her housekeeper came in.

'Mr Harrington telephoned this afternoon, Miss Markham. He'll be at his London home after six and would like you to call him.'

So Roger was back. He worked for the European Commission and most of his time was spent in Brussels. But he rang her frequently and had not given up hope of resuming their affair.

'Sorry to leave you alone again, Luke,' she murmured.

He shrugged and raised his whiskey glass to her. 'I dare say Gilly and I will be gone by the time you're back, so have a restful evening.'

'Thanks.' Swinging on her heel, she returned to her bedroom, though there were three telephones downstairs she could have used.

'I know it's short notice,' Roger apologised when he came on the line, 'but I came over unexpectedly to see the minister and wonder if you're free tonight?'

'I am,' she said instantly, seeing him as a welcome distraction from thinking about Luke. 'I'll take a cab and meet you in town.'

'You're an angel. That will give me time to take a catnap. I've been up since dawn. Make it Gavroche at eight-thirty.'

Determinedly Andrea set out to look her best. She had never been conceited about her looks, and once Abraham had moulded her into the image he wanted, she had not given further thought to it. But since Luke had come back into her life she had become aware of the power that beauty gave a woman, and that it was a mask behind which she could hide her true feelings. No one seeing her tonight, elegant in a black lace slip of a dress and dramatic scarlet cloak, would guess she was torn with jealousy to think of Luke dining with her stepsister.

Roger had not seen her since Luke had performed his Svengali act on her, and he was bowled over by the transformation.

'I'd better get re-assigned to London,' he said as they settled at their favourite table. 'I wouldn't trust any man with you now.'

'It isn't the men you have to trust,' she teased. 'It's me!'

'I'd trust *you* with my life.' His brown eyes were intent on her. 'You already have my love.'

'Oh, Roger, please don't go on hoping.'

'I'll hope till the day you marry someone else.'

Misty-eyed, she stretched out her hand to him. In looks he was the typical English diplomat: tall, thin, with light brown hair, precise features and a calm manner. But to those who knew him well he was a warm, caring, humorous man. If only she could have fallen in love with him instead of... Frightened, she refused to finish the sentence.

'After dinner, let's go dancing,' she said abruptly.

'Good idea. Then I can show you off some more!'

As if aware of her inner turmoil, Roger set out to capture her attention, regaling her with amusing anecdotes about various Euro-ministers. Andrea did her best to enter into the spirit of the evening, but couldn't stop wishing it was Luke sitting opposite her; Luke who was paying her such wild compliments; Luke who was looking at her as if she were the only person in the world with whom he wanted to be.

It was after two before the evening ended and she could finally close the front door and be alone. Trying to forget one man by going out with another didn't work for her, she conceded as she wearily went upstairs, and she'd do well to remember it.

Passing the door of Gillian's room, she could not resist opening it a crack. Without surprise she saw it was empty, and the all too familiar pang of jealousy shot through her. Where was Gillian's sense? She knew Luke played the field—dammit, she'd broken off their engagement because of it—yet now she was willingly walking the same path again.

Perhaps Luke was right and it *would* be better if Gillian found somewhere else to live when they returned from the concert tour—even if she herself had to finance it. At least what the eye did not see, the heart would not grieve.

But no, that wasn't true. Whether or not she saw Luke, she would always grieve for him, grieve for the love she could not allow herself to give him, the children she could not bear him.

It was an annihilating admission and ripped away the pretence she had laid over her emotions from the day she had met him again. At last she faced the truth: she loved Luke; had loved him since she was a teenager, though she hadn't been fully aware of it. She recalled how her heart had raced at sight of his dark hair and broad shoulders; how ashamed she had been of her body's response to his brotherly goodnight hug, knowing he was going to marry her stepsister.

And he still might, she thought bitterly.

'Forget him and count your blessings,' she chided herself. 'Why pine for a man who'll never be faithful to one woman? You have your music, your public, your fame. That's more than enough.'

Is it? her inner voice cried. Wouldn't you gladly trade them all to be Luke's wife—even if he ended up breaking your heart?

CHAPTER NINE

ANDREA did not see Luke until the end of the following week, when she returned to the St John's Wood studio to hear her finished album, and found him already there, talking to Hugo. She had not been surprised by his silence, Gillian having told her he was in America, where a young protégée of his was making her operatic début.

'It's so boring when he's away,' Gillian had complained. 'He's the most exciting man I've ever met.'

'I imagine many other women say the same thing about him,' Andrea had reminded her drily, a comment which Gillian had ignored.

Seeing Luke after an absence, Andrea found him more dynamic than ever, and no one would have guessed from his gleaming silver-grey eyes and clear skin that he had flown in that very morning from New York.

'You seem to make a habit of flying back from abroad to be at my recordings,' she commented with a cool smile.

'A manager's duty—except that this duty is also my pleasure.'

She glanced at Hugo. 'Are you pleased with the recording?'

'Delighted. But you have the last word, of course.'

Silently they sat down to listen. As always when she heard herself play, Andrea found it difficult to believe she was the pianist. It was as if she were listening to a stranger; but a stranger who made her hypercritical. Yet today there was nothing to criticise. As Hugo had said, the play-back couldn't be faulted.

'You're right, Hugo,' she smiled. 'I'm very happy with it. Do you have a sleeve design to show me?'

'Yes. Luke's already chosen it.'

'Suggested,' Luke corrected quickly. 'Andrea has the final word.' Rising, he crossed over to the table and placed his hand on a folder lying on it. He waited for her to join him before opening it to disclose some half-dozen mock-ups for the cover.

Now she knew why he rated Jack Lenton so highly as a photographer. Each mock-up displayed a different portrait of her: smiling, serious, pensive, joyous; each one capturing the very essence of her personality, though until this moment it was a personality only her parents and Abraham had known.

'Which one do you want to use?' Luke murmured.

'I'm not sure I want to use any of them.'

'Don't you like them?'

'Oh, yes,' she admitted. 'But they give away too much of me.'

He studied the portraits again. 'Yes, I see what you mean. But don't you also give yourself away when you play?'

'No. I interpret and disclose the composer, not myself.'

'Maybe you *should* disclose something of yourself. Why be afraid of showing your emotions? You know the saying: as you give, so shall you receive.'

'Not always,' she answered curtly, wondering what his reaction would be if she disclosed the tempestuous emotions *he* aroused in her.

'My God!' he exclaimed. 'If every teenager who had an unrequited crush on a guy behaved as you do now, there would be a hell of a lot of repressed women around!'

Astounded, she stared at him, then realised he had misunderstood her remark. And thank goodness he had! Better for him to think she had been harking back to the past than to the way she felt today.

Lowering her eyes, she studied the mock-ups again, picked up the one where she was smiling warmly into camera, and swung round to show it to Hugo.

'That's the one Luke chose!' he smiled.

'Shows what good taste he has!' Returning to her chair, she collected her purse. 'If that's all the business for today, I'll be going.'

'I've set up some Press and radio and TV interviews for you,' Luke advised, following her out.

'I don't like being interviewed.'

'Because they always ask why you've only given one public performance?' he challenged.

'Yes, if you must know,' she flared. 'And I'm sick of it!'

'Well, you'll now be able to tell them you're doing a European concert tour and will end it by playing at the Festival Hall.'

The very thought made her tremble, and seeing it, Luke frowned.

'Don't worry about it, my dear. I know you collapsed halfway through your last concert, and the papers blew it up into some sort of phobia, but you must ignore it.'

How could she ignore it when she was petrified she might do the same thing again? Andrea wondered, and nearly told him as much. Yet if she did, and he cancelled the tour, Bella would be the one to financially suffer.

'A few weeks from now you'll be proving the papers wrong,' Luke continued.

'I can't wait,' she lied, quickening her step.

'May I drive you home?' he asked.

'I'm not going home.' Andrea said the first thing that came into her head, unable to bear being alone with him.

'Then I'll take you where you're going.'

'It's out of your way. I'll get a taxi, thanks.'

'Meeting your married friend?'

She swallowed hard, then knew she had to give him some explanation. 'It isn't what you imagine. He's the husband of a—a friend, and they're having marital problems. He thinks I can help him smooth things over.' It was close enough to the truth, she decided, and hoped Luke believed her.

'Why didn't you tell me this to begin with?' he questioned.

'Because you irritated me by jumping to the worst conclusion!'

To her surprise, a flush stained his cheeks. 'I'm sorry, Andrea. Will you forgive me?'

'Of course.'

'Prove it by having dinner with me tomorrow.'

To refuse again would increase the tension between them, and knowing this was unwise in view of the concert tour, she nodded. 'Very well.'

'Your enthusiasm is overwhelming!' he said drily. 'Let's hope that by the end of the evening you'll feel differently. Anywhere particular you'd like to go?'

'I'll leave it to you.'

He waited with her until she found a taxi, and as he closed the door she sank back against the seat with a sigh of relief. She had a day's grace to prepare herself for their date. Would she manage to keep her cool and hide her feelings for him? If she didn't, he'd do his best to seduce her, and in her present state of tension she could well end up as another notch on his belt.

It was a relief when the taxi dropped her at the hotel where Peter had been staying. He had gone to Holland yesterday, and when he had telephoned to say he was posting her a letter giving her his itinerary, she had asked him to leave it at his hotel in case Gillian saw it and recognised his handwriting.

Paying off the taxi, she went in to collect it, then sat in the lounge while she copied in her diary the hotel names and dates where he would be staying.

Strolling down Bond Street in search of a taxi—it was still rush-hour and they were hard to come by— she was tempted to drop into a theatre to see a show. It was better than staying home brooding. But the thought of leaving Gillian alone decided her against it, and when a taxi drew up a few yards ahead to deposit a passenger, she took it as a sign, and hailed it.

So much for signs! she thought an hour later when Mrs Prentice informed her that Gillian had gone with Mr Kane to a recital at the Barbican. It also explained why his invitation to *her* had been for tomorrow and not tonight. Would her stepsister pretend to enjoy the concert, she wondered, and had Luke forgotten she had always loathed classical music? Or maybe it didn't matter to him.

The evening dragged by. Usually Andrea enjoyed her own company, but tonight she was too restless to relax, and asking Mrs Prentice to delay dinner, she soaked in a hot bath, lavishly pouring in her favourite bath oil. It did the trick, and, feeling more human, she slipped into a new housecoat, a gift from Bella on her last birthday. Oyster-pink silk, full-skirted, with a tightly fitting bodice and narrow but deep cleavage, it wasn't the type of garment you wore to prepare toast and porridge! No, this one called for candle-light and wine and the touch of a man.

She almost tore it off, then stopped herself. To do so would be defeatist: an admission that Luke was the only man for her. And he wasn't. Somewhere, some time, she would fall in love again. If she believed that strongly enough, it would come true.

After dinner she switched on to the last half of the Barbican concert. The music was magnificent, but spoiled for her by the mental image of Luke and Gillian sitting side by side, listening to it. She was leaning forward to turn off the radio when the door opened and they walked in.

'I thought you were at the concert?' she cried, jumping to her feet.

'We were, but Gillian wasn't feeling well,' Luke explained.

'It's only tiredness,' Gillian said quickly, forestalling any questions. 'I'll be fine when I've had a good night's sleep.'

'Don't forget to take your pills,' Andrea said automatically.

'I'm not an invalid,' Gillian snapped, and stalked out.

'I could do with a brandy,' Luke murmured into the silence.

'Help yourself.'

As he strode across to the drinks trays, Andrea moved away from the sofa where she had been sitting—she didn't want Luke joining her there—and curled up in an armchair, shaking off her slippers as she did.

'What happened to Gillian tonight?' she asked.

'Beats me. She was fine when I collected her, then during the interval she started shaking and said she felt terribly cold, so I suggested we leave.' Luke settled in the corner of the sofa. 'I've an idea you're keeping something from me. What exactly's wrong with her?'

Wishing she could be honest, but knowing her stepsister would be furious if she was, Andrea skated as near to the truth as possible. 'She—she had a nervous breakdown and isn't quite over it.'

'Then is it wise to let her go to Rome with you?'

'It's better than her staying here alone.'

'What caused her breakdown? Her broken marriage?'

'I—er—don't know.'

Luke frowned and sipped his brandy. 'At least I'm not responsible for *that*.'

'True. But resuming your relationship with her isn't helping the situation. She's extremely vulnerable right now and can be easily hurt.'

'I am not "resuming" my relationship with Gillian—as I have made clear to her. I feel she needs to be taken out of herself, and I've offered her my friendship. Nothing more.' He set down his glass and leaned forward. 'I hope you believe me?'

His grey eyes sought hers, then moved lower, making her aware of her plunging neckline. Abruptly she leaned further back in her chair, and seeing his mouth twitch, knew he had noticed it and was amused.

'You do believe me, don't you?' he reiterated.

'Yes, I do,' she replied, surprising herself. 'But it isn't always what one says that counts. It's what the other person assumes.'

He frowned. 'I thought I was helping her, but obviously you don't agree; so I'll take note of your comments and make myself less available—diplomatically, of course. I don't want to hurt her ego.'

'Just make sure she knows you're dating other women too,' Andrea said lightly. 'It won't surprise her—given your reputation.'

'Is that why you finally agreed to have dinner with me?' he mocked. 'Because you see yourself as the sacrificial lamb?'

'Hardly. Fond though I am of Gillian, some things are too big a sacrifice! I decided to go out with you because it seemed sensible to maintain a truce, bearing in mind the coming tour.'

'And here I was, hoping you fancied me.' His cool appraisal raked her from head to curled-up feet. 'I find *you* extremely fanciable.'

'What a pity you aren't my type.' Her heart was thumping like crazy but her drawling voice belied it. 'I prefer blond men.'

To her annoyance he laughed and rose lithely. 'Time to go, I fear. I'll see myself out.' Pausing at the door, he glanced back at her. 'Blond men or not, our date tomorrow still stands.'

Not until the sound of his car died away did Andrea turn off the lights and go to her room. Had Luke believed what she had said? After all, it was a popular male view that women often said no when what they wanted was to be persuaded to say yes.

Well, in twenty-four hours he would probably put her statement to the test. She prayed she would pass it with flying colours!

CHAPTER TEN

ANDREA was so apprehensive about her dinner date with Luke that it was hard to concentrate on her usual daily practice; nor was she helped by Gillian who, apparently forgetting that she did not like anyone in the music-room when she was working, kept drifting in to chat.

'Don't you have anything to do today?' Andrea finally burst out.

'I'm going to Brighton after lunch. I'm staying with Jackie overnight.'

'Jackie?'

'The girl I went to see a couple of weeks ago. We were at secretarial college together.'

Knowing Gillian would soon be out of her hair decided Andrea to forget music for the rest of the morning, and she suggested they go for a walk on Hampstead Heath.

It was good to get into the fresh air and she set a brisk pace. Soon both of them were breathing hard but feeling all the better for it.

'Luke told me he was taking you out to dinner tonight,' Gillian said in her most casual tone. 'I thought you couldn't stand him?'

'It's business,' Andrea found herself excusing. 'We'll be thrown together during the tour, and being friendlier seemed expedient.'

'How wise of you! I hope you keep it up after the tour's over.'

'That won't be necessary. I'll be parting from him then.'

'I wish you'd reconsider that. It could make things awkward for me.'

Deliberately Andrea did not answer, silently acknowledging that unless a way could be found of distracting Gillian's attention away from Luke, her marriage was doomed, despite his assertion that he now regarded her solely as a friend. Dammit, he was a virile man and unlikely to turn down an affair if it was offered to him.

Andrea thought of this again as she dressed later that evening, trying on and discarding a Ralph Lauren black chiffon shirt and matching silk palazzo trousers—she felt it might be too formal, given Luke's casual manner of dress—in favour of an emerald-green Armani shift. Excitement, which she could not dampen however hard she tried, made her eyes glow like amethysts, and she deliberately refrained from emphasising them with anything other than mascara, unwilling for Luke to think she had gone to any trouble over her appearance. Because of this she also wore no jewellery other than her customary Rolex Oyster watch.

At eight o'clock she was waiting for him in the drawing-room, sipping a glass of white wine and glancing through the evening paper. At half-past she thought Luke had stood her up—perhaps to pay her back for the many times she had rejected him—and was on the point of going to her room to change into casual trousers when she heard his car draw up in the drive. Hurriedly she sat down and picked up her wine glass, and was the picture of relaxation as Mrs Prentice announced him.

To her surprise he sported a suit, though the loose, oversized jacket in stone linen owed more to Paul Smith than Savile Row. Beneath it, a white jersey sweater complemented the casual style, and made him appear younger and light-hearted.

'A puncture,' he explained succinctly, holding up dirt-stained hands to prove it. 'Do you mind if I clean up?'

At her nod he disappeared, returning several moments later, when she handed him a whiskey.

'No water and heavy on the ice,' she smiled.

'Just what the doctor ordered.' He drained half of it at a gulp. 'I've had a long, hard day, and changing a tyre was the last thing I needed.'

'Couldn't you have called a garage?'

'Then I'd have been even later.'

'I thought you'd decided not to come.' Her smile was meant to show she was joking, but he did not smile back.

'I'd have come if I'd had to crawl here on my hands and knees.'

'Such an answer deserves this.' She proffered a silver dish of popcorn, and he gaped at it.

'You remembered?'

'That you liked it better than nuts? How could I forget when you used to eat it by the bagful?'

'I'm glad you're beginning to remember the fun things, not just the bad,' he said, popping some into his mouth.

Andrea avoided his eyes. 'I've many happy memories of our friendship, Luke. It's a pity they were overshadowed by our quarrel.'

'I did apologise at the time, if memory serves me right.'

'By sending me an LP of Beethoven's Second Piano Concerto.'

'Do you still have it?'

'No.' She'd choke before confessing she had found it impossible to part with it, and that it had accompanied her wherever she had lived from her student days onwards.

'Which means you didn't accept my apology,' he commented.

'Sending a gift is an easy way out.'

'I realise that now, and I'm sorry. I guess I saw you as a kid who'd be placated by a present, and when you weren't, I——' He hesitated, then bit the bullet. 'I assumed that your loyalty to Gillian was stronger than your friendship with me.'

This was dangerous ground and she drew back from it by changing the subject. 'Where are we having dinner?'

'At Luigi's.' He named one of the best Italian restaurants in London. 'As I remember, you were a pasta *aficionado* as a teenager.'

'I had little choice. It was all you could afford!'

'We can go somewhere else if you prefer.'

'I'm still a pasta freak!' she assured him.

'Then let's go.'

During dinner, her fear that they would have nothing to talk about except music disappeared as their conversation ranged over books and films, politics and philosophy, and it wasn't until they reached the coffee stage that Luke referred to the interview he had arranged for her the following week: two on television, two on radio, and an in-depth profile in an erudite Sunday paper.

'Isn't it a bit much?' she queried. 'The public will be sick of me.'

'Hardly. You're witty and intelligent and a delight to the eye.'

'You sound as if you're quoting from a publicity hand-out!'

'I am—the one I've just written for you!'

She laughed, and he leaned forward and touched her arm. 'I should make you laugh often. It's a lovely sound. Sexy yet demure.'

'That's a contradiction of terms!'

'Which is why it's so attractive. A seductive woman who's also a demure girl.'

'Hardly a girl,' she protested. 'I'm twenty-five.'

'You look younger.'

'But *you* know I'm not. That's one penalty of our past association. You know everything about me.'

'If only that were true!' His look was steady as a probe. 'But you're an iceberg, Andrea. Two thirds of you is hidden below the surface.'

'Stop fishing, Luke. I have no secrets.'

'I doubt *that*. Everyone has the odd skeleton in their cupboard.'

'What's yours?' She came back at him so fast that he chuckled: a warm sound that she found as fascinating as the way his looks had changed now he was relaxed. Yet he still exuded strength and virility, and she knew he was a man it was dangerous to underestimate.

'Like you, my life's an open book,' he stated. 'But fire off your questions and I'll answer honestly.'

She hesitated, though it was a mere pretence, for she knew exactly what she wanted to find out. 'You once said you have all my recordings, so that means you've seen many photographs of me, yet how come you didn't recognise that I was really Annie Jones?'

'Because of the extraordinary change in your appearance—and also because I had no idea you were serious about playing the piano professionally. Why didn't you tell me? You gabbed nineteen to the dozen about everything else!'

'I didn't want you to think I was taking advantage of our friendship, and expecting a helping hand.'

'But that's what friends are for.' He sighed. 'And I *was* your friend, Andrea. I didn't see you just because you were Gillian's little sister. I found you funny and sweet and I enjoyed your company. As I do now.'

It was impossible not to be pleased by the obvious sincerity of his words, and as the evening went on and she was further bombarded by his wit and charm, her resistance reached melting-point. No wonder women fell over themselves to please him and give him what he wanted, and how easy it would be for her to do the same!

What would he be like as a lover? Covertly she studied him as he sipped the last of his wine, his eyes narrowed in concentration as he appreciated its depth and fullness. So would he appreciate a woman: savouring her, responding to her different moods and skilfully enhancing them. He might not be husband material, given his roving eye, but as a no-strings-attached lover he would be perfect.

'Emerald-green suits you.' His words demanded her attention, and with relief she concentrated on them.

'It's the first time I've worn it. I was talked into it by a persuasive saleslady.'

'She must have been good—knowing how obstinate you are!'

'I'm not in the least obstinate.'

'You could have fooled *me*. I bet you don't see yourself as an innocent either.'

'I certainly don't, and my success proves it.'

'I wasn't alluding to your career. In that respect you're on the ball. But on the personal side you're Sleeping Beauty!'

'Waiting for Prince Charming's kiss to awaken me, I suppose?'

'Precisely.'

Boldly she went on the attack. 'I hope you don't see yourself in the role?'

'Well,' he teased, 'I think I could awaken you.'

'Only think? I expected a more positive response!'

'When the time and place are right, you shall have it,' he promised softly.

'Stop flirting with me, Luke! It's a useless exercise.'

With a shrug he gave his attention to the dessert menu he had just been handed by their waiter. 'I'll have the *crème brûlée*,' he said after Andrea had ordered raspberries and *crème fraîche*, then added when they were alone again, 'If I can't have you, I must try another way of satisfying my craving for something sweet!'

'I'm glad you can find compensation so easily!'

His chuckle gave Andrea the distinct impression that she was playing with fire; an impression that gained credibility when he suggested having coffee at his place instead of the restaurant.

'Jack Lenton sent me all your contact prints this afternoon, and I want you to look at them,' he explained.

'At least that's more original than etchings!' she couldn't resist saying.

'That sounds as if you don't trust me,' he challenged.

'Give me a reason why I should.'

'I can't think of one for the moment!'

It was Andrea's turn to chuckle, and it hid her nervousness as she went with him to his car. Within five minutes they were at the four-storeyed neo-Georgian house in Grosvenor Street that served as his office and residence. His apartment was on the top floor, reached by a small, mirrored private lift that led directly into a pale green entrance hall.

Andrea was painfully aware of the heavy beating of her heart and was hard put not to turn and run. Snap out of it, she chided herself as she preceded him into the living-room. You accepted his invitation knowing he was going to make a pass at you, and if he does you've only yourself to blame.

'Do you approve?' he asked, and she turned a startled face to him. 'Of the room,' he explained, his sweeping arm encompassing it.

'Oh, yes. Yes, very much,' she said hurriedly, giving it her attention.

It was vast—large enough to hold forty with ease—and was divided from the dining area by a central fireplace pier, faced on both sides with aluminium. To balance this emphatic design feature, deep rectangular pilasters, stopping just short of the ceiling, flanked the large bay window at the seating end. These contained audio-visual equipment, with inset speakers at a high level. Long, low sofas covered in creamy-beige raw silk were ranged round the room, forming several conversation areas.

In one corner was a Bechstein baby-grand piano, and she couldn't help wondering how many famous musicians had given private recitals here.

'None,' came the surprising answer when she voiced her thoughts. 'When I invite anyone to my home, it's always in a personal capacity, and I'd no more expect a musician to play for me than I would expect a free consultation from any doctor or lawyer who happened to be a guest.'

'I wish everyone was like you. I often get asked to play when I visit friends and I always feel guilty if I refuse.' Andrea went to the keys and lazily ran her fingers along them. 'I assume it *is* used from time to time?'

'Quite often. It's my relaxation.'

'I didn't realise *you* played,' she said in surprise.

'Very badly,' he smiled.

She couldn't imagine his doing anything badly, but didn't say it. 'Why not let me be the judge?' she challenged.

'OK. But it won't be classical. I refuse to suffer by comparison with my illustrious clients!'

He lowered himself on to the stool, and Andrea perched on one of the Mies van der Rohe chairs near by. Without preamble he launched into a feisty rendering of Scott Joplin's 'The Entertainer'. It was far from a simple piece, and in spite of his modest words he was, as she had suspected, very accomplished. As he came to the end she gave him a well deserved round of applause. His performance had been flawless and she said as much.

'It's a piece I play often,' he shrugged. 'I'm a bit of a ragtime *aficionado*.'

'So am I,' she confessed. 'I suppose that surprises you?'

'Because you're a classical pianist and shouldn't like anything else? Credit me with sense! I'm delighted you aren't a musical snob.'

They smiled at one another and he rose and came towards her. 'How about that cup of coffee I promised you, or would you prefer a liqueur?'

'Any more alcohol and I'll fall flat on my face!'

'If you'd said flat on your back it might have been worth my while to secretly lace your coffee!'

'Don't tell me you prefer your women drunk and incapable?'

'When my looks and charm don't get me anywhere, I'm prepared to resort to other means!' The teasing lightness of his voice showed he was continuing the verbal game they had been playing all evening, but she knew it was his way of disguising the mounting sexual tension between them, a tension that was increasing with every passing moment.

Silently she followed him into the streamlined kitchen. An informal dining area was sited at one end, and plain white units with a dark wood strip and matching wood floor were offset by white tiles, effectively grouted in dark blue.

'Decaffeinated or the real stuff?' he enquired, taking a gold glass cafetière out of a cupboard.

'The real stuff. I know it's poison, but I'd rather live a shorter life and enjoy my coffee!'

'My sentiments entirely. Go into the living-room and make yourself comfortable while I prepare it.'

'I'd rather stay here and watch you.'

'Scared I might add that secret something after all?'

'Frankly—yes!'

He laughed. 'I'm too intimidated by you to try!'

'A likely story!' She watched as he ground the coffee beans and set two cups and saucers on a tray. Not being particularly domesticated herself, she was surprised how much at home he appeared to be in the kitchen.

'Is your cooking as good as your coffee?' she enquired when they were finally sipping it, seated at opposite ends of one of the long, low couches in the living-room.

'Better! Come for dinner tomorrow night and I'll prove it.'

'I imagined you with a live-in chef,' she said, studiously ignoring the invitation.

'You imagined right,' he confessed disarmingly. 'But I can rustle up a fair meal myself when pressed.'

'A man of many accomplishments. Any other things I don't know about?'

'I can think of one.' His voice was husky. 'If you're interested I'd be happy to enlighten you.'

His meaning was obvious and his eyes made no attempt to conceal his desire to bed her. From the moment she had accepted his invitation to see the photographs she had known she would be faced with such a decision, and while she didn't doubt he genuinely had the photographs, it had not been the real reason he had asked her here. It had simply been a plausible excuse, and she had gone along with it so that, if necessary, she could pretend she had really believed him. But she wanted Luke as much as he wanted her; had done so from the moment they had renewed their relationship.

Yet past experience had taught her that sex for its own sake was not enough for her; she needed involvement on an emotional level as well. Momentarily she closed her eyes. Face the truth again, she ordered herself. You *are* emotionally involved with Luke even though he doesn't know it, and though making love to her would just be a passing pleasure for him—she was too much of a realist to kid herself he might be in love with her—for her it would be the first time she had made love to a man she whole-heartedly cared about.

But he must never know it, and for this reason she had to play it cool, so cool that he would believe she regarded it as lightly as he did. If he guessed that she cared for him he might try to talk her into a more permanent affair, and for her this would be the worst possible scenario, for the longer their physical union, the greater would be her hope that he might decide to make it a lasting one. And what a wasted hope that would be! No, a one-night stand mightn't be easy to salve with her conscience, but at least she would be left with a memory to treasure, and not spend the rest of her life wondering what she had missed.

'I *am* interested, Luke,' she whispered, finally answering his question, and smiling as she did, her amethyst eyes showing nothing of her innermost feelings.

'How I've longed to hear you say that,' he said huskily, rising lithely to his feet and drawing her into his arms. 'I'd almost given up on you, Andrea. Darling Andrea.' Her name was almost like a prayer on his lips, stifled as his mouth came fiercely down on hers.

This time she offered no resistance, and arching her body, leaned into him. Feeling her pliancy, his lips softened and moved over hers with a long, slow warmth that gradually took possession of them both. Her mouth parted beneath his and she trembled as his hands caressed her body, extending the intimacy of the kiss.

'This is no place to make love,' he said thickly, and picking her up as if she weighed no more than a child, headed for the bedroom.

As he set her down he loosened his hold to unfasten the buttons of his shirt, and she began unzipping her dress. But he reached for her again and turned her round, slowly sliding the zip all the way down to the base of her spine. Eyes darkened by desire, he stepped in front of her again and watched the dress slither to the floor in a rippling fall of silk, revealing creamy white skin and the softly rounded contours of her body, barely covered by two wisps of black lace.

'Exquisite,' he murmured, gazing at the gossamer web that scantily veiled the soft rise and fall of her breasts. Delicately he caressed the rounded curve, then let his finger trail higher to the velvety nape of her neck. 'There's a tiny vein beating in your throat,' he went on, his voice growing huskier. 'It's fluttering like a moth over a flame. I wish I could catch you as easily and keep you captive.'

With tantalising slowness he removed the two brief barriers, heightening the anticipation for them both by prolonging the final unveiling. As anticipation turned into realisation and she stood naked before him, luminously etched in the pool of light coming from the lamps either side of the king-sized bed, he was content to enjoy the full beauty of firm, tip-tilted breasts, the subtle curve of hips, the slender length of shapely legs.

Surprisingly Andrea felt no embarrassment, no inhibitions, and met his gaze fearlessly. How intent his eyes were, the irises enlarged by the dimness of the room.

'You don't know how long I've been waiting for this moment,' he said, his voice deep as he swiftly removed his clothes, dropping them into a heap next to hers, while she followed every movement, longing for him, aching for him, yearning for fulfilment.

Swinging her into his arms again, he carried her to the silk quilted bed, the ivory sheets already turned enticingly back. He placed her gently upon them, then came down beside her, skin touching skin.

Andrea drew a shaky breath, revelling in the feel of his flesh, the warm masculine scent of him, infinitely erotic, instantly arousing. Her slender fingers stroked his dark, thick hair, then glided down his neck to his bare back. She felt the powerful surge of his manhood, and marvelled at its size and pulsating strength.

'Touch me,' he murmured, running his tongue along the edge of her lips where the two curving lines met. 'Hold me, sweetheart, hold me here.'

Luke guided her hand between his strong thighs, and she slowly caressed him in a gentle, rubbing movement. He was like molten rock sheathed in silk; hot, hard and sleek. God, how she wanted him, wanted him inside her, right now, this very moment.

But he refused her urgent plea, quieting her with his hands and mouth as he cupped her breasts, rolling and rubbing her nipples between thumb and forefinger before taking each tip in turn between his lips, nibbling, suckling, teasing each one to tingling erectness.

Every part of her became alive beneath the masterly skill of his touch, bringing her to such a wanton peak of desire that she begged him to come into her. But he went on caressing her with hands and lips and tongue, searching out every curve and indent, every hollow, until she was crying for the mercy of release from the fiery passion consuming her.

'I want you!' she cried. 'I want you!'

Only then did he move on top of her, his swollen organ sliding effortlessly into the hot, dark wetness between her thighs. Gripping him with her legs, she absorbed him into her, knowing this was what she had been waiting for all her life.

'Easy,' he warned. 'I'm on fire for you, so go easy.'

'No. I want you now. I can't wait!'

Spurred by her words, Luke groaned deep in his throat, an involuntary sound that she echoed as he began rotating his hips, plunging deeper into her, each thrust longer and more piercing. Andrea's grip on his hot, leaping muscle intensified, and he groaned again and thrust urgently forward, his hands hard beneath her buttocks.

As the pace increased, Andrea lost control, carried away on a storm of passion that erupted her into space and sent her soaring to the stars. For mindless time she burst the bounds of reality, a sensual, quivering mass of feelings without thought, passion without cessation, desire without end until gently, as if she were a feather moving in slow motion, she drifted back into her body and became conscious of Luke's.

Later, as dawn streaked the sky, they touched, caressed, pleasured with hands and mouth, and made love again. Andrea clung to Luke, digging her nails into his flesh, raking them against his skin, groaning his name as he pummelled relentlessly into her. But at the moment of release, as he flooded her with the sweet juices of his arousal, she knew that whatever the future held for her, she would have no regrets for tonight.

How could she, when it was a memory she did not wish to erase?

CHAPTER ELEVEN

FLYING high above the Alps, with Gillian in the seat beside her, Andrea glanced down at the snow-capped mountains, suddenly excited by the thought of returning to Rome, where she had studied so happily several years ago. Byron's words came into her mind: 'Oh Rome! my country! city of the soul!'

And so it had been for her; the beauty and majesty of it opening her heart to a religious experience whose profundity remained with her to this day. She drew on it now, finding it calming her spirit and helping her distance herself from the coming ordeal of her first public concert since she had run off stage in tears four years ago.

She was still calm when they landed at Fiumicino Airport, though Gillian was effervescent with excitement as they waited by the conveyer belt for their luggage.

'I bet you'll be mobbed by the paparazzi when we get outside,' she exclaimed. 'I hope I get *my* photograph in the papers too.'

'Not today you won't. My flight was booked under my real name, so the bloodhounds don't yet know I've arrived.'

'That's stupid. Don't you want publicity for your concert?'

'Sure I do. But Luke's secretary told me he's arranged a Press party for this evening, which will be a whole lot better than being torn to pieces at the airport.'

'Trust Luke to be on the ball,' Gillian said happily.

'It's his job to be,' Andrea retorted. 'It's what I'm paying him for!'

It was a less than fair comment, but she had not seen him since the night they had made love, and knowing he was waiting to meet her in the arrival hall had set her nerves on edge. Guilt at the manner in which she had left his bed swamped her, and futilely she wished she could turn back the clock. Yet at the time she had thought she was doing the right thing...

After they had made love again at dawn, and how infinitely satisfying his slow taking of her had been, Luke had cradled her in his arms and fallen asleep again. But she had forced herself to stay awake and, as his hold on her had eased, she had carefully slipped out of bed, gathered up her clothes and dressed in the living-room.

She had been unable to leave without tiptoeing in to see him. Asleep, he had looked defenceless, the strong mouth softened into gentleness, face slightly flushed from their lovemaking, his hair slightly ruffled, making him appear younger and unexpectedly vulnerable. If only he loved her as she loved him. If only he were capable of faithfulness. For a poignant moment she had allowed herself to believe that this was possible, then memory of his behaviour when he had been engaged to Gillian had forced her to see him as he was, and not as she would like him to be, and with heavy heart she had walked out.

She wanted the memory of their night together to be unmarred by any argument that might have ensued had she told him she would never go to bed with him again. Indeed, given the strength of her feelings for him, she had been scared that face to face she would not have convinced him she meant it. So she had left a brief message scrawled in lipstick across the mirror above the double marble vanity unit in the bathroom.

Great night. Just how I like it! No obligations, no commitment. Like you, I prefer variety, so no repeat performance.

Designed to stop him pursuing her, it had the desired effect. Contact during the following weeks had been via Alan Bradly, his second in command, who informed her that unexpected commitments made it impossible for Luke to accompany her to her television and Press interviews, as planned, and that he would be escorting her instead.

Andrea had gone out of her way to show she had no objection to Alan's company. Tall and tow-haired, he could more easily have been taken for a lifeguard on a Californian beach than a budding musical entrepreneur, and she was not surprised when a couple of newspapers linked their names and hinted at a romance.

'I hope you aren't annoyed by it?' Alan questioned anxiously. 'We can issue a denial and——'

'What's the point? No matter what we say, they won't believe us. If you're embarrassed by it though, we *can* make a statement.'

'Embarrassed? You've got to be kidding! Being linked romantically with you is doing my image a power of good!'

'Here are our cases.'

Gillian's voice interrupted Andrea's reverie, and she followed their porter through Customs and into the arrival hall. She saw Luke instantly, as did Gillian, who rushed forward to kiss him.

'It's good to see you looking so relaxed,' he greeted Andrea without embarrassment as he disengaged himself from Gillian's embrace.

She gave him a brief smile, her body seemingly made of jelly as her senses absorbed his bronzed skin and shiny dark hair, his tall frame casually garbed in open-necked white cotton shirt and beige trousers. No wonder feminine eyes hungrily followed him. But he appeared oblivious of their admiring looks as, in fluent Italian, he instructed the porter to take the luggage to a waiting limousine.

There was nothing in his behaviour to Andrea to show that the last time they had been together they had made passionate love, and the tension that had been gripping her eased. Clearly, he had decided to behave as though nothing untoward had happened between them. He knew the pressures on her and, clever businessman that he was, obviously had no intention of doing anything to jeopardise the tour.

'You studied here, didn't you, Andrea?' he said after they had been driving for a while.

'Yes. And I loved every minute of it.'

Memories crowded back as they passed the ruins of an ancient aqueduct arching across the landscape—a relic of ancient Rome's excellent water system—before joining the great stream of traffic entering the heart of the capital.

Their car slowed to a crawl as they approached the famous Via Vittorio Veneto, giving them time to stare at the pavement cafés whose tables were filled with tourists sipping drinks under brightly coloured umbrellas. Gillian chattered and exclaimed at every changing scene, but Andrea soaked up every detail in silence, vowing that come hell or high water she would find time to go on a lone prowl through the familiar streets.

Their hotel was situated in a quiet spot beyond the city, and set amid velvet-smooth lawns and colourful gardens.

'I thought you'd find it more peaceful here,' Luke murmured as they stepped into a plush lobby, with plants cascading down the walls and water flowing into a large corner pool.

Andrea wished she could as easily find inner peace. But all she was aware of was her coming public ordeal. Her breath caught in her throat and sweat erupted on her forehead, making her quickly turn away her head as the manager guided them down a wide, airy corridor to a suite of two bedrooms separated by an elaborately furnished sitting-room. It was filled with flowers, and standing on the bar was an enormous basket of exotic fruit.

'With the compliments of the hotel, Signorina Markham,' he smiled. 'We will do everything in our power to make your stay a happy one.'

'Why don't you two take things easy until this evening?' Luke suggested when they were alone. 'The Press conference and party aren't till seven, so you have plenty of time to unwind.'

'I'm going down to the pool,' Gillian said. 'Can you join me?'

'Sorry,' he apologised, walking to the door. 'I've too much to do.' He glanced at Andrea. 'Need anything?'

Only you, she longed to say, but instead she shook her head and went into her room to unpack. She was still putting away her clothes when Gillian came in, a brightly patterned thigh-length cotton jacket masking a matching swimsuit.

'Shall I wait for you?' she asked.

'No. I'll join you later. But watch out for the sun. It's more potent than you get in Brighton!'

'But not as potent as you get in Australia!'

With a cheery wave Gillian disappeared, and Andrea pondered for the umpteenth time whether she might have been willing to indulge in an affair with Luke had her stepsister not come back into his life.

'No, I wouldn't,' she said aloud. Gillian was a consideration, but her own feelings were the overriding factor, and given Luke's feckless emotions, a relationship with him could only end in unhappiness.

In an attempt to stop thinking about him, she decided to go for a swim.

Emerging from the lift at the lower-ground floor, she came out of the shade into brilliant sunshine. Twenty yards away, glinting like an aquamarine beneath the Roman sky, was a large curved pool, surrounded by brightly coloured mattresses and lounging chairs, all occupied.

Her stepsister was on a sunbed at the far end, and Andrea was delighted to see a spare lounger beside her.

'When I came out here I thought I'd have to sit miles away,' Gillian informed her. 'But as soon as I gave the

attendant our room number he showed me over here.
Luke must have arranged it.'

Andrea gave him full marks for foresight, even
though it confirmed her suspicion that he was trying to
anticipate her every wish to ensure she was as free of
anxiety as possible. Did he know of her phobia? The
real reason she had never given public performances?
He hadn't said so, but... She frowned. No, only
Abraham knew about it, and he had never told anyone.

Dropping her towelling robe, she dived into the water, ferociously swimming four lengths before climbing
out.

'I don't remember you being such a good swimmer,'
Gillian remarked admiringly.

'I wasn't until a few years ago,' Andrea replied, pat-
ting herself dry. 'But then I decided I needed the exercise.'

'I'm glad to hear you don't spend *all* your time at the
piano,' an unmistakably deep voice interjected.

Andrea turned sharply to see Luke smiling down at
her. A short blue robe accentuated his colouring and
exposed his strong, sinewy legs. Dropping down at the
edge of the pool, he shrugged it off, and Andrea longed
to run her fingers over the silky skin of his shoulders.
They were the colour of mahogany and had a natural
sheen that needed no oil.

'So you managed to get away after all?' she quizzed.

'Where there's a will there's a way! You're both so
ravishing, I thought you'd need protecting from the
Italian men!'

'Gillian's in more danger than I am,' Andrea responded. 'They're strongly attracted to blondes.'

'So are most other men!' Gillian giggled. 'Don't you agree, Luke? Most of the Hollywood sex symbols are blondes.'

'If you're trying to give me a complex, you're succeeding!' Andrea said lightly, putting a hand to her dark curls. 'I'm clearly destined to be an old maid.'

'If you are, it will be from choice.' Though Luke was smiling, it did not reach his eyes.

'I'm going for a swim,' Gillian announced. 'Coming in, Luke?'

'I'll race you both.' He raised an eyebrow in Andrea's direction, but she shook her head.

'Great,' Gillian cried, and grabbing his hand, pulled him into the pool with her.

As a contest it was a joke, for he was a powerful swimmer and, in a few strokes, was yards ahead. But halfway down the pool he checked speed and allowed the slender blonde figure to pass him, only putting on a burst of activity as they neared the far end, but leaving it so late that he could not win.

'What's the winner's prize, Luke?' Gillian asked, brown eyes wide and innocent as they rejoined Andrea.

'How does a bottle of champagne sound?'

'Delicious,' she cooed, running her fingers across the damp whorls of hair that curled on his chest.

Andrea was seized with such a fit of jealous rage that she could cheerfully have drowned them both. Instead she lay stomach down on the lounger and unhooked her bikini top. A little while later she heard the popping sound of a champagne cork, then felt the light touch of Luke's hand on her shoulder.

'Not for me, thanks,' she said, correctly interpreting it. 'Alcohol at this time of day gives me a headache.' It wasn't true but she could not help being perverse. Luke's impersonal affability was beginning to grate on her. 'I'd rather have a *citron pressé.*'

As he gave the order to a passing waiter, she reached her hands behind her to fasten her top. The two ends slipped from her grasp, and she was fumbling for them when she felt Luke's hands draw them together and hook them closed.

'Too shy to go topless?' he enquired behind her.

'No—just cautious.' Sitting up, she swivelled round to sit cross-legged on the mattress. 'You never know where the paparazzi are hiding, and baring my all wouldn't create the image I want with my public.'

'It might get you an even bigger public!'

'Not the sort I want.'

He didn't dispute her comment but studied her silently and without expression, making no pretence of doing otherwise. With an unconcern she did not feel, Andrea did the same to him. Except that it was damned hard to maintain indifference, for the sheen of bronzed muscles, set off by the most minimal of briefs, set her pulses leaping. With a superhuman effort she made her expression bored and turned her eyes away from him.

'This is the life,' Gillian said into the silence as she raised her glass in Luke's direction. 'Here's to a fabulous holiday.'

'It may be one for you,' he smiled, 'but it's hard labour for Andrea and myself.'

'I don't see why. All the concerts are booked and travel arrangements made, and I'm sure Andrea doesn't need to practise any more. If she does, she'll get stale.'

Andrea couldn't help laughing. Gillian was sometimes so ridiculous that it was impossible to get angry with her. 'You're so right,' she said humorously. 'I'll sunbathe all day and waltz into the concert hall to rattle off my pieces each evening.'

Knowing she was being teased, Gillian pouted and flopped down on the mattress beside Andrea, then smiling provocatively at Luke, removed her scarlet bikini top, exposing small, pointed breasts.

'I'm thinking of having an implant.' She swivelled her body from side to side to afford him a better view. 'Do you think I need it?'

'No. You have lovely breasts,' came the matter-of-fact answer. 'But even if you didn't, you'd be crazy to have an unnecessary operation.'

'But don't you think they're too small?'

Abruptly Andrea lay flat on the mattress again, blocking her ears to Luke's reply. She was disgusted by Gillian's behaviour and suddenly wished she had allowed Peter to confront his wife, as he had wanted to do. Ill or not, she should face her husband and accept the truth of the accident, instead of being allowed to run away from it. Yet Dr Marshall had been so adamantly against it. Sighing, Andrea closed her eyes and pretended to sleep.

To her astonishment she managed to do so, and did not awaken until she felt the pressure of a foot on her stomach. Opening her eyes, she saw Luke's wide-shouldered frame towering over her.

'You'd better go and change. You've had enough sun for one day,' he stated.

'I'm well aware of how much I can take,' she answered coolly, moving into a sitting position. 'Where's Gillian?'

'Gone up to the suite. Said she was going to order tea.'

'Don't let me keep you.'

'You aren't. But I've already told her I'll be tied up with phone calls for the next few hours.'

'In that case, I *will* go in.' Andrea levered herself up, ignoring Luke's helping hand.

'I'll see you to your door,' he said as they walked towards the hotel.

'No one's likely to kidnap me *en route*.'

'More's the pity. If today's an indication of how you're going to behave on tour, I wish they would! You've been acting like a bitch from the moment we met at the airport.'

'Then ask Alan Bradly to stand in for you. He's done a great job these past few weeks.'

Luke's breath hissed between his teeth. 'So that's it?' He stopped walking and forced her to do the same. 'In view of the message you left on my bathroom mirror, I thought you'd prefer not to see me for a while. So I obliged.' The wide mouth thinned. 'I thought I was doing you a favour. You said you liked variety and Alan's an attractive man.'

Andrea's face flamed. 'I don't need anyone to pimp for me, Luke, or is that part of your service too?'

Luke swore softly under his breath, though sufficient words were audible to make the depth of his anger clear. 'A one-night stand was your choice, Andrea, not mine. Remember that.'

She tried to think of a cutting reply but none came to mind. All she could think of was the pain and joy of seeing him again, and of the effort she must make not to let him know it.

'Let's leave it, shall we?' she said, turning away from him. 'I'll see you at the Press conference.'

Side-stepping him, she ran down the path into the coolness of the hotel, and not waiting for the lift, raced up the stairs.

CHAPTER TWELVE

ANDREA decided on a black jersey camisole shift for her Press conference, ruefully conceding how much Luke had changed her attitude towards fashion.

Wickedly short and deceptively simple, her dress relied on the curves of the wearer to show off the cleverness of the cut. The same could be said of her hair. Gavin had decided to cut it shorter when she had gone to him last week, and it now curled round her head like osprey feathers, showing off the rounded perfection of her skull. Several fronds curved forward on to her cheekbones and the hollows of her cheeks, while slightly longer tendrils caressed her ears, where she clipped diamond and amethyst earrings that matched the narrow necklace round her neck.

Her almond-shaped eyes glowed like the luminous heart of a pansy—darkest indigo with a hint of violet—and eschewing eye shadow, she brushed mascara on to lashes so long and thick that most people thought them false. Her small mouth, with its full lower lip, was coloured crimson, but after surveying it she wiped it off with a tissue and applied a delicate pink that made her lips look soft and moist and infinitely kissable.

Would it evoke memories for Luke? she wondered. Remind him of their hours of love, when their mouths had nibbled and sucked and drunk of each other's sweetness as their bodies became one? Desire gripped her and she fought it off, knowing that this way lay madness. Luke was not for her; not for any woman who wanted faithfulness and commitment.

Repeating this like a litany, she went down to the flower-filled conference-room he had booked for tonight. It was empty save for some waiters who were busying themselves at the bar, and Luke, who was studying a printed list in his hand. As if he had sensors in the back of his head, he swung round and strode towards her as she came in.

'You're early,' he smiled. 'No one's arrived yet.'

'Shall I go away and come back later?'

'Only if my company bores you!'

'Stop fishing,' she said lightly, then couldn't help adding, 'I wish I didn't have to meet the Press. They always ask such personal questions.'

'Don't worry about it. I'll be here to field them.'

She nodded, aware of his gazing at her throat.

'A gift from an admirer?' he asked.

'No. I bought it myself.'

'It's beautiful. And so is the dress. It will have all the men pawing the ground!'

He handed her the Press list he was holding, and she saw that every music critic of note in Rome had been invited, as well as gossip columnists and members of the foreign Press. Had Abraham been managing her she would have dreaded the next hour, but Luke's presence gave her a confidence she had never had before, though this didn't lessen her horror at the concerts ahead of her.

'I get so tense at the idea of playing in public,' she confided tentatively. 'All those faces watching me... I'm not sure I can do it.'

'Of course you can!' he retorted instantly. 'Look straight into the auditorium and think of everyone there as friends stretching out their hands to you.'

Stretching out their hands... It was the worst thing he could have said and she trembled with fear. Outstretched hands were the hands of the teenage boys who'd surrounded her in the park all those years ago. If only she could remember what had occurred. But the harder she tried, the further it receded.

'Where have you gone, Andrea?' Luke's voice dragged her back to the present. 'Women aren't usually *distraite* when they're with me. I must be slipping!'

'Only where *I'm* concerned.' With an effort she regained control of herself, abandoning all thought of confiding in him. 'I just happen to be immune to your charm!'

'I can remember a few hours when you weren't.'

Colour flooded her cheeks and she was achingly conscious of his nearness. She drew back a step but his hand came up to clasp her elbow and she felt the hardness of his fingers. Her eyes were on a level with his chest. His black suede jacket was undone and through the open neck of his silk shirt she saw dark curling hair. It elicited a more intimate memory and she shook her head to dislodge it. What was wrong with her? Being suggestive was second nature to him and meant nothing, yet as soon as he touched her she was reduced to a quivering lovesick teenager. Firmly she edged back, and he took the hint and released her arm.

'Andrea!' Gillian bore down on them, blonde hair a mass of tiny curls, slender form ethereal in floating chiffon ruffles. A couture dress without question, and the latest fashion too, so it must be another present from Luke.

'Why didn't you tell me you were leaving the suite?' her stepsister went on.

'Because you were resting.'

'Well, Roger's calling you from Brussels. I left him hanging on the line.'

'Good heavens!' Andrea moved forward, unexpectedly stopped by Luke's arm.

'I'll have the operator transfer the call here,' he said.

'No, thanks. I'd rather take it in my room.' She sped away, so relieved to escape that her voice was full of warmth when she spoke to Roger. 'How thoughtful of you to ring. You're definitely Chaucer's idea of a knight!'

'Not a successful one at the moment. I've been trying my best to get to your Rome concert but I can't make it,' he apologised. 'Forgive me, darling.'

'I'm almost glad you won't be here. The way I feel now, I'm not sure I'll be able to go through with it.'

'That's nerves speaking!'

'It's more than that.'

'What do you mean?'

She went to answer, then stopped. How to convey a fear when she didn't know what the fear was? Anyway, it wasn't something she could discuss on the telephone.

'I'll definitely be at your London concert,' he went on, 'even if I have to resign from my post!'

'I won't hold you to that,' she said, and determinedly kept the conversation light until he rang off.

Returning to the conference-room, she found it teeming with people and throbbing with the mellifluous tones of Italian. A smoothly handsome man from a Milanese arts journal instantly approached her and backed her into a corner.

'We're doing a profile of you in our next month's issue,' he informed her in heavily accented English, 'and there are a few personal questions——'

'Hold them,' Luke intervened, materialising from nowhere, much to her relief. 'We're having a question-and-answer session shortly and you can ask them then.'

Forestalling further comment by the simple expedient of drawing Andrea away to meet someone else, Luke remained firmly at her side until he had introduced her to all the leading columnists in the room, after which he led her over to the podium at the far end.

Instantly all talk ceased and everyone focused on her. Her breathing quickened and the room receded and advanced. Then Luke began speaking, and as everyone concentrated on him instead, she managed to gain control of herself.

He gave a brief résumé of her career for the sake of the less well informed, and then threw the floor open to questions. They were easy to handle and her confidence grew as she even managed to field several relating to the fact that she was still single. She was silently congratulating herself on how well she was doing when a stern-faced young woman asked her the one question she had been dreading.

'Why is it that you haven't given a concert tour until now?'

'I—I was too busy recording,' she stammered.

'But you haven't appeared on a concert platform in England either,' the woman persisted. 'Is there a personal reason why you avoid playing in public?'

'Personal?' Andrea repeated, trying to give herself time to come up with an answer. 'I don't follow you.'

'Do you suffer from an illness that makes you nervous of appearing on stage?'

There was a noticeable buzz of interest in the room as everyone stared at Andrea with new eyes. Could there be a human-interest angle they had been missing all these years?

Andrea fought for breath, feeling a scream building up inside her and petrified that she wouldn't be able to contain it. She searched for the door but it was miles away and she knew she would explode before she reached it.

'Relax,' Luke whispered, swiftly drawing her close so that she felt the warmth of his body seeping into her. 'I'll deal with this.'

She leaned against him, trembling, and gradually became aware that he was talking.

'There are always personal reasons why an artist prefers one form of artistic self-expression to another,' he explained, enumerating several famous musicians who hadn't performed on the concert platform. 'But now that Miss Markham has embarked on this tour, I assure you it will be the first of many—as long as she isn't put off by telephoto lenses trying to snap her in the bath!'

There was general laughter, and as it died away he invited everyone to help themselves to food from the buffet, a suggestion that resulted in a minor stampede.

'There's no reason for you to stay here any longer,' he murmured to her. 'Slip away and I'll meet you upstairs after I've chatted up a few more people.'

Gratefully Andrea did as she was told, and as she headed for the lift she was joined by Gillian.

'If that pack of newshounds in there is the price of fame,' the older girl said, 'I'll stick to being a nobody!'

'You can't blame them for being curious. It's part of their job.' Andrea was magnanimous with relief now that the ordeal was over.

'When that old biddy asked her question, I had a fit in case you told her the truth.'

'I would have done, if I knew what the truth was. But I don't.'

'Then for heaven's sake why not forget it?' Gillian burst out as they entered their suite. 'Why must you keep imagining the worst? Forget it,' she reiterated.

'Do you think I haven't tried? After the débâcle of that first concert I spent months with a psychiatrist. I even went to a hypnotist but it didn't do any good. When I'm in a crowd, when I know a lot of people are watching me, I panic.'

A low moan escaped Gillian's lips, and seeing how pale she had grown, Andrea instantly regretted her outburst. 'I don't blame you for it, Gilly. You were a kid yourself and had no idea I wouldn't be safe in the play-ground.'

'You're a darling for saying so, and I love you for it. But I shouldn't have left you, and I'll regret it all my life.'

Giving her a quick hug, Gillian ran from the room, and Andrea sank into an armchair and closed her eyes, emotionally exhausted. She was aroused from a light doze by a tap on the door, and sleepily opened it to find Luke on the threshold.

'Sorry if I awoke you,' he apologised as she stifled a yawn.

'That's OK.' She returned to her chair. 'Help yourself to a drink.'

'Not until I've eaten. I thought the three of us would go out to dinner. I can promise you the best ravioli in the world!'

'Count me out. All I feel like is bed.' Seeing the sudden thrust of his lower lip, she felt a tide of colour race into her cheeks. 'That wasn't an invitation to join me!'

'I didn't imagine it was—not after the message you left for me when you walked out of my apartment. It wasn't a very friendly thing to do.'

'I wanted to set the record straight.'

'You certainly did that. For the first time in my life I felt I'd been used.'

Her head tilted sharply. 'I dare say quite a few women could say that to *you*.'

'On the contrary,' came the soft answer. 'Whenever I've made love to a woman it's been because of a mutual desire. As it was with us. You won't deny that, I hope?'

'Of course not.' How could she when she had responded so passionately?

'Then why the brush-off?'

Schooling her expression—she dared not give away the crazy emotions racing through her body—she gave a casual shrug. 'It causes complications to mix business with pleasure.'

'I'll remind you of that when the concert tour is over.' His mouth curved provocatively as he noted the question in her eyes. 'I promised to release you from your contract then, if that's what you still wanted, and if you do, it will leave me free to——'

'No! What happened between us was something I don't want to repeat.'

'Why not, Andrea? For me, it was a wonderful experience, and I could have sworn it was the same for you.'

At that moment she would have given anything to know why he was being so persistent. It wasn't because he lacked other women, of that she was sure. So was it because his ego couldn't tolerate a rebuff, or did he still believe that if they were lovers she would remain his client?

'Hi there, Luke!' Gillian glided into the room, fresh as a daisy. 'Have the newshawks gone?'

'Yes.'

'Luke's come to take you out to dinner,' Andrea interpolated.

'Both of you,' he stated.

Andrea shook her head. 'I told you, I'm too tired.'

'Luckily I'm not.' Gillian slipped her arm through his. 'May we go dancing afterwards? I've heard Rome's full of fantastic nightclubs.'

'We'll see,' he answered non-committally.

'Have a good time whatever you decide to do,' Andrea said, and feigning a yawn, retired to her room.

Slipping into a comfortable wrap, she wandered on to the balcony and looked out over the lawns towards the hills where dark cypresses—so typical of the Italian landscape—were interspersed between luxurious villas and apartments. The sky, tinged with pink, was growing darker as the sun set, and a few hotel guests were strolling in the gardens. A young couple paused to kiss beneath a tree, and Andrea felt such a pang of loneliness that she stepped hastily inside.

As she did, there was a knock on the door and a waiter called out, 'Room service!'

'I haven't ordered anything yet,' she informed him, opening the door and seeing him prepare to push in a trolley.

'It's with Signor Kane's compliments,' he said.

Astonished, she took in the champagne bottle set in a bucket of ice, the silver dish filled with caviare, the warm toast wrapped in a snow-white napkin, and a bowl of peaches and raspberries so fresh that the bloom still lay on them.

The waiter wheeled the trolley over to the window, placed a chair beside it, and left. Only then did Andrea notice the sealed envelope propped against the crystal jug of cream. It bore Luke's handwriting, and with trembling fingers she opened it and took out the single sheet of paper. He wrote,

> Yes, I'm being bossy again, but that's because your well-being matters to me. Enjoy!

The note was signed 'L' and she traced it with her finger. What a charmer he was. But she was too canny to be taken in by it, aware that beneath the charm was an ambitious, calculating man who used women either for amusement or for the promotion of his career—in her case, possibly both.

Tearing up the note, she dropped it in the waste-paper basket, then sat down and forced herself to eat. The fact that Luke had sent it wasn't going to stop her enjoying it! As the delicious grains of caviare melted in her mouth, washed down by the driest of champagne, she was reminded of her student days in Rome, and the café on the Via Cavour where she had gone most evenings for a cheap meal.

Suddenly she had an overwhelming desire to escape from the opulence with which she was surrounded, and wander through some of her old haunts in the poorer parts of the city. No sooner had she thought of it than she ran into her bedroom, changed into a simple cotton dress and comfortable sandals, grabbed her purse and left the hotel.

Hailing a taxi, she instructed the driver to take her to Trastevere, the older part of Rome across the Tiber, where she had once lived. The man looked surprised, and when he finally crossed the river was reluctant to leave her in such a run-down area.

'Be careful, *signorina*. There are plenty of villains round here.'

'I'll keep to the main thoroughfares,' she promised.

Walking slowly, and jostled by many scruffy individuals, she searched out some of the restaurants and shops she had known, feeling strangely exhilarated when she found one. But for the most part they had changed hands, and some no longer existed.

The bandits had long since gone from the once notorious thieves' quarter, and many of the shabby façades were now handsomely restored. Reaching the Ponte Sisto, she paused halfway over to look down on the sluggish, dull green waters of the Tiber, and reflected on the pleasure of wandering through Rome.

She had no fear of being here alone, and because of this forgot the taxi driver's warning and the promise she had made him. Hearing the sound of splashing water, she saw it came from a fountain set in a cobbled square at the end of a narrow alley. As she went on looking at it, the cloud that had been obscuring the moon drifted away, and the fountain glowed as if made of silver. Enchanted, she hurried towards it.

The alley was deserted, as was the square, but the moon bathed it with friendly light and she peered with interest at the beautifully carved stone cherub from whose mouth water spouted into the coin-filled pool below. Behaving like a typical tourist, she opened her bag and searched for a few lire to throw in. As she watched them join the pile at the bottom, she heard footsteps behind her and, swinging round, saw three grinning young men bearing down on her.

'American, Eenglish?' one questioned with a heavy accent. 'You very preetty.'

As they surrounded her, clearly intent on preventing her escape, she was assailed by a fear so strong that she was immediately plummeted back to her childhood self and the youths who had tormented her in the park. Her mouth went dry and she moistened her lips.

'Please leave me alone,' she said in fluent Italian, speaking with as much composure as she could muster. Except that no composure was evident in the reedy voice that emerged from her throat. 'I'm s-sightseeing with friends, and—and if I scream they'll come running.'

Laughter greeted this statement and they moved closer to her. She was conscious of the heat emanating from their bodies, and her nostrils prickled at the smell of stale sweat and even staler garlic. Instinctively she backed away, feeling the rough stonework of the fountain rubbing her skin through the thin fabric of her dress, and painfully conscious that there was nowhere she could run.

The tallest of the three reached out a large hand and placed it on her shoulder. 'You lovely lady,' he leered, pushing his stubble-dark face close to hers. His lips pursed and Andrea, with terror-induced bravery, pushed her knee hard into his groin.

Yelping with pain, he doubled up, and with all her strength she shoved him against one of the other men, slipped through the gap this made, and ran hell for leather down the alley, not stopping until she reached the safety of the brightly lit main street, bustling with pedestrians and traffic.

Gasping for breath, she searched for a cab, almost crying with relief when she finally found one. What a fool she had been to ignore all the rules of safety. She had behaved as irresponsibly as Gillian, who had left her in the playground to go boating with her new boyfriend. But, as on that occasion, God had been watching over her and nothing had happened.

For a moment it didn't sink in, then, heedless of what the driver might think, she gave a whoop of joy. Nothing terrible had happened to her tonight, and nothing terrible had happened to her in the park that long-ago day! She had not been molested, as she had always imagined, and if Gillian hadn't made her swear not to tell their parents about the boys, she might, in discussing it openly, have realised that, and saved herself from having her life blighted for so many years.

It wasn't until she was back in the quiet of her hotel suite that she realised that this revelation would put an end to the dreadful panic attacks she suffered when in a crowd. Joy filled her, permeating every fibre of her being, and she longed to share her happiness with someone, but other than Abraham and Gillian, nobody knew of the trauma that had kept her off the concert platform.

Joy gave way to loneliness, and as she wandered round the room, filled with lovely *objets d'art*, baskets of flowers, bowls of fruit and chocolates, she knew she would never find total fulfilment in her career. She needed a man to love; one who would love her in return and share the rest of his life with her. And though Luke would happily satisfy the first part of her need, he was incapable of satisfying the second.

Lowering her head in her hands, she wept.

CHAPTER THIRTEEN

NEXT morning, Andrea received a brief note from Luke saying he had to leave Rome for several days. Her relief was mixed: delight that she could lower her guard and give all her energies to rehearsing for the concert, yet also a deep longing to hear his voice and feel the spell of his nearness.

The city was in the middle of a heat wave, and though the hall was air-conditioned, the temper of Manuel Sanchez, the conductor, heated the atmosphere, so that by the end of each day she was drained and would happily have settled for a quiet dinner in her room. Yet this was her stepsister's first time in Rome and, feeling guilty at leaving her alone most of the day, she made the effort to take her out in the evenings.

'Where shall we go tonight?' Gillian asked as Andrea entered the suite. 'One of the waiters at the pool said Albertino's is the best restaurant here.'

'Then I doubt we'll get in at such short notice,' Andrea replied, stifling a yawn. 'But there's no harm trying.'

'Will you do it? My Italian's non-existent.'

Andrea had her hand on the receiver when a knock on the door heralded Luke's return, and with an excited cry Gillian rushed over and hugged him.

'Darling, I'm so pleased you're back! We're just seeing if we can get in to Albertino's.'

'In a month, if you're lucky. It's the "in" place at the moment. But if you'll both have dinner with me, I——'

'Andrea's worn out and wants to stay in,' Gillian intervened. 'She was only coming out tonight to humour me.' Deep brown eyes widened at him. 'You've neglected us horribly the past few days. Where were you?'

'In Tokyo. One of my artists had an accident and I went there to give him moral support.' He glanced at Andrea. 'Martin Ibbot,' he explained.

'I read about it in *The Times*.' Andrea was amazed she sounded so calm when her pulses were racing with joy at seeing him. 'I didn't get the impression it was serious.'

'We deliberately kept it low-key, but there was a real chance his playing days were over.'

'My God!' Andrea sank on to the nearest chair. This was every artist's nightmare. 'Is it—is he . . .?'

'He'll be fine, though he'll need months of physiotherapy.' Luke rubbed the side of his face in a weary gesture that made her aware of how exhausted he looked. 'Promise me one thing, Andrea: don't try prising open a can of sardines with a knife!'

'You said he'll recover,' Gillian cut in impatiently, as she always did when Luke was speaking to Andrea. 'So don't let's dwell on what might have been.' She moved towards her bedroom. 'How dressy is the place we're going to? You didn't say where you're taking me.'

'Where you wanted to go,' came the casual answer.

'Oh, you angel, I adore you!'

The door closed behind her and Luke raised an eyebrow in Andrea's direction. 'Will you adore me too, now I've a table at Albertino's?'

'Afraid not,' she said lightly.

He came a step closer to her, and though she kept her breathing shallow, the spicy warmth emanating from him filled her lungs and tingled through her body.

'Are you really too tired to have dinner with me?' he quizzed softly, looking so genuinely disappointed that she wasn't sure if it was real or feigned. Yet one thing she *did* know: she no longer intended being a party to her stepsister's deceit. It was time Gillian came clean with him and told him she was still married! Once she had, it was up to Luke what he did.

'That table at Albertino's *is* rather enticing,' she murmured, deciding that it was also time Gillian didn't have things all her way. 'Perhaps I'll feel brighter when I've had a shower. Can you give me half an hour?'

'No problem. I'll help myself to a drink and unwind.'

'You're the one who should be having an early night,' she said before she could stop herself. 'You dash all over the place like a kite in the wind!'

His eyes narrowed. 'Worrying about me?'

'Naturally. An exhausted manager isn't a good one!'

'I'd be good for you regardless of how exhausted I was.'

Certain he wasn't talking of management, she turned tail and fled, the soft laugh echoing behind her, telling her she hadn't misunderstood him.

When she finally returned to the sitting-room she was surprised to find Luke alone.

'Pity Gillian doesn't take after you,' he commented.

Aware of his watching her, she sat down, resisting the urge to pull at the hem of her short-skirted purple dress.

'I understand the rehearsals are going well,' he went on.

'Who told you?'

'I spoke to Manuel Sanchez every evening. He praises you to the skies. I chose not to talk to you,' he went on, seeing her lips tighten with anger, 'because I know how uptight you are at the coming concerts and I didn't want you to think I was checking on you.'

'Then why are you now admitting that you did?'

'Because I've a gut feeling you've conquered whatever it is that's been bugging you. Am I right?'

He leaned towards her, his black silk-mohair jacket falling back to show a form-fitting white silk shirt, through which the matt of hair on his chest was easily discerned. Memories rushed in on her, threatening to swamp the control she was fighting so hard to retain. How rough his hair had looked when she had lain against him, yet how soft it had felt to her touch; as soft as the skin that she had explored with her mouth, breathing in its warm, musky scent even as her tongue had lapped the fine dew of desire from it.

'Well?' Luke continued. '*Have* you conquered your nerves?'

'I...' She moistened her lips. 'It wasn't—isn't—nerves.'

'Don't play semantics with me. Just give me a simple answer.'

'There isn't a simple answer,' she said crossly. 'People can't be slotted into grooves like bits of a jigsaw. They are complex, multi-faceted. And I've no idea how I'll react when I face an audience again.' She jumped to her feet, body shaking. 'That's the awful part. Waiting to find out, and knowing that if I run off stage this time, I'll never play in public any more.'

'So what?' he said calmly, leaning back in his chair and touching the tips of his fingers together. 'You can concentrate on TV recitals and recordings, and you'll still be as famous and successful.'

Astonished, she stared at him. 'Then why did you insist on my doing this tour?'

'I wanted to make you have another go at conquering your nerves or phobia or whatever it is you're suffering from. If you can, great. If not...' His shoulders lifted. 'The important thing is that you tried.'

She went on staring at him, seeing him in a new light. Not as a taskmaster intent on earning as much from her as possible, but as a man who wanted her to face her fear and overcome it. In that instant she decided to tell him the truth.

'It isn't nerves or a phobia. It's——'

'Sorry to be so long,' Gillian cried, rushing into the room. Startlingly lovely in white chiffon that showed off her tan to perfection, she pirouetted in front of him. 'How do I look?'

'Good enough to eat—that reminds me, I'm starving, so let's go!'

Gillian glanced at Andrea. 'Such a pity you're too tired to...' Her voice trailed away as she took in the dramatic purple taffeta dress and high-heeled pumps on the long, shapely legs. 'You're coming with us?'

'Luke talked me into it,' Andrea said sweetly, trying not to laugh at the dismay on the pert face in front of her. If truth was told, she *was* tired, and would rather have gone to bed—preferably with Luke, her treacherous thoughts added—than dine out in a public restaurant, the focus of curious eyes. But it was worth the effort just to see her stepsister's annoyance!

Albertino's was as excellent as its reputation, and they dined sumptuously at a table set in a large bow window overlooking a superb view of the River Tiber, dark and gleaming below them.

Luke was obviously a valued customer here, given the way he was treated by the staff, and Andrea thought how well his casual air of style and understated manner suited these patrician surroundings.

They all chose fish of one kind or another, and she was content to let Gillian monopolise the conversation, for it gave her the chance of watching Luke. He seemed to prefer black suits to those of any other colour, and tonight his shirt had a narrow red stripe that exactly matched his Gucci leather-belted trousers. Thank goodness he eschewed the ubiquitous gold chain and medallion, and favoured the slimmest, most unobtrusive of watches; nothing so obvious as gold, but twenty-first century titanium! As he studied the wine list, head on one side, well-shaped hands resting on the table-cloth, her love for him washed over her with such force that she knew he would always have a place in her heart.

'We're in luck, they've an '83 Montrachet,' he murmured as the wine steward left them.

'One of my favourites,' Andrea confessed. 'I love it. It's crisp yet has a lovely aroma.'

'So has a good croissant. Do you love those too?'

She laughed, seeing the point he was making. 'OK, I *like* it. Is that better, sir?'

'Yes. Love is a word that's constantly abused. As is "genius" and "brilliant".'

'How true,' Gillian simpered. 'Though "genius" and "brilliant" apply to *you*.' ·

'You're too flattering,' Luke grinned. 'I think of myself as a businessman with a flair for what I'm doing. No more than that, I assure you.'

Andrea longed to disagree with him. Gillian had exaggerated his abilities, but he had definitely understated them. Still, in view of their current relationship, she had no intention of praising him.

It was past midnight when they left the restaurant, and though Gillian suggested they go on somewhere to dance, Luke pleaded fatigue.

'I bet he's up to his old tricks,' she said waspishly when he left them at the door of their suite.

'You mean seeing other women?' Andrea ventured.

'What else? He seems to have cooled off me, or haven't you noticed? If he hadn't, he'd have called me from Japan.'

Andrea was tempted to ask how involved they had been before he had gone away, but since she didn't want to hear the answer, she shrugged. 'I've been so busy with rehearsals that I haven't noticed anything else.' She feigned a yawn. 'Night, Gilly. See you tomorrow.'

Not surprisingly, Andrea wasn't able to get Luke out of her mind. In London he had declared he wasn't in love with Gillian and had denied that he had resumed their relationship. Yet Gillian acted as though they had. Yet even if she was telling the truth, Andrea knew she had only to say the word for Luke to turn to herself.

As dawn pinked the sky she debated whether she was being foolish not to accept what he had to offer her. After all, these days fifty per cent of marriages weren't permanent! And who knew? Even given his track record, she might be the one woman capable of holding him. It was an enticing supposition, but before she could fall for its blandishments, logic warned her against it. A leopard didn't change its spots, and she was far more likely to end up as one more notch on his belt. It was this fear that would always stop her from saying yes to him.

But when she walked into the coffee shop and found him there, silky dark hair gleaming, eyes sparkling and his whole aura emanating vitality, it was all she could do not to throw herself into his arms.

'I thought you'd be having breakfast in bed,' he smiled, rising as she joined him.

'I forgot to order it last night, and it meant a twenty-minute wait. What about you?'

'I only have it in my room when I've someone to share it with.'

Fury engulfed her and she could cheerfully have killed him.

'I'm single, Andrea, and I've never claimed to be celibate,' he added, correctly reading her expression. 'But nor am I the Lothario the gossip columnists make out.'

'You don't need to excuse yourself to me,' she shrugged.

Silently he buttered a croissant, tucking into two while she nibbled a piece of toast and drank a cup of coffee.

'Croissants are my weakness,' he confessed, seeing her expression as he took a third on. 'I love them.'

'As much as I love Montrachet?'

For an instant he was puzzled, then he grinned. '*Touché*. Hung by my own nit-picking!'

Acknowledging this, she rose. 'I must be off. I've a final rehearsal and I don't want to be late.'

'Hang on while I sign the bill. I'm coming with you.'

'There's no need.'

'Don't be silly.'

Accepting that she had been, she fell silent as he accompanied her across the lobby to a waiting taxi.

It was only as she entered the concert hall that she realised she had not experienced the usual feeling of dread at the sight of her face on the giant hoardings plastered around the outside, advertising the recital. Nor did the usual butterflies appear when she crossed the platform to take her place at the piano. The real test would come tomorrow night, of course, when the auditorium was filled and she was faced by a live audience, but even this thought did not bring on the usual sense of panic.

Her session with the orchestra went on for the better part of the day, and though Luke occasionally disappeared to make telephone calls, most of the time he sat in the fifth row of the stalls next to the manager, Carlo Andretti, and some of the office staff. When she played the last note of the symphony for the last time, they rose and joined the orchestra and conductor in a warm round of applause.

'Your hours of practice have paid off,' Luke assured her as they drove back to the hotel late that afternoon. 'You appeared totally confident.'

Once more she longed to explain why; to tell him of the traumatic happening that had haunted her since she was a child, the end of which had buried itself so deep in her subconscious that she had never been able to exhume it until a few nights ago, when three young men had surrounded her in the alley near the Ponte Sisto and she had miraculously remembered she hadn't been molested, as she had always believed, merely bullied and terribly teased.

Yet fear kept her silent; the fear that bringing her trauma into the open—even though she now knew it had been a false one—would bring the phobia back. Perhaps it was better to say nothing until tomorrow night was successfully behind her. At least then she would know if she had finally conquered the past.

'I thought you'd like to know that the tour's completely sold out,' Luke said, breaking into her thoughts.

'You're joking?'

'Haven't you been reading the papers? They've been singing your praises all week.'

'I deliberately haven't looked at them in case they said anything bitchy and it upset me.'

'A couple of articles might well have done,' he conceded. 'They suggested we might be more than business associates.'

'That's hardly surprising, considering your reputation!'

His mouth curved in the semblance of a smile, though she saw it did not reach his eyes. 'Care to know how one journalist dubbed us? The Rake and the Vestal Virgin.'

Andrea tossed her head. 'At least you've found out I'm not!'

'True. And very——' he paused delicately before continuing '—very interesting it was too. Pity we can't repeat it.'

Again fury kept her silent. Interesting, was it? Damn him for making it sound as though she had been some experiment. Yet maybe she had been! The seduction of the cool, sarcastic woman who had idolised him as a teenager. What a feather in his cap to bring her to heel. Triumph coursed through her at the knowledge that he hadn't succeeded. Oh, he had seduced her all right, but she had turned the tables on him by making him believe she hadn't wanted him as more than a one-night stand!

'What are your plans for this evening?' Luke questioned as they reached the hotel.

'Dinner in my room and an early night. Definitely.'

'A lull before the storm?'

'With Gillian around, there won't be a lull!'

'I'll take her off your hands,' he offered immediately. 'Tell her to meet me in the lobby at eight.'

How adroit he was, using her desire for peace and quiet as an excuse to get Gillian on her own again. She gave him a saccharin-sweet smile of thanks. 'You're so thoughtful.'

'Anything to keep my favourite client happy!'

'And your bank balance in the black!'

'Of course.' He paused as they reached the lift. 'Excuse me if I leave you here. I've just seen someone I want to have a word with.'

Gillian was delighted when Andrea relayed Luke's invitation, and hurried off to have her hair set, seemingly forgetting the accusations she had made against him last night. But then, as his ex-fiancée, she knew better than anyone else that he wasn't the faithful type!

It was a relief when eight o'clock came and she had the suite to herself. After a leisurely bath and a light meal, she went to bed. But sleep was impossible. Images of a blonde head close to a dark one danced before her eyes, and when she managed to expunge them their place was taken by a picture of the concert hall filled with people, hands outstretched to her.

Shaking, she ran into the bathroom and searched for some Nembutal. Better a drugged sleep than no sleep at all.

CHAPTER FOURTEEN

Unused to sleeping-pills, Andrea did not awaken until ten o'clock next morning.

Too edgy to remain in her room, she decided to go for a stroll. A stealthy peek into Gillian's room showed her still asleep—heaven knew what time she had returned last night—and she seized the opportunity of going out alone to enjoy this most beautiful of cities.

It was a lovely morning, without wind or clouds to mar the luminous light that etched the Roman skyline in sparkling clarity, and for several hours she wandered the streets, finally finding herself by the Spanish Steps, one of her favourite haunts when she had lived here. Contrary to their name, the steps had been a gift from France, their only connection with Spain being that the façade of the Spanish embassy had been designed by the same architect!

Making her way down them, she saw that nothing had changed. Hordes of young people still congregated here, regarding it as their meeting place, and many were supplementing their funds by selling cheap jewellery. Remembering her own hard-up days, she purchased a few trinkets, knowing her housekeeper's teenage nieces would be delighted with them.

Sitting on the steps, soaking up the sunshine, she watched the paparazzi who swarmed in the square at the bottom, hoping to snap pictures of unwary celebrities.

Luckily they didn't connect the slender young woman in faded jeans and T-shirt with the svelte, exquisitely dressed Andrea Markham, and she was able to enjoy their antics without being disturbed.

But inevitably the thought of her concert destroyed her peace of mind, and she decided to return to the hotel. Going in search of a taxi, she was enticed by the smell of freshly cooked ravioli coming from a small trattoria, and she went in to treat herself to some. The little room was filled with exuberant students, who, thinking her one of them, quickly made a place for her.

It was almost two-thirty when she let herself into her suite and was immediately pounced on by a white-faced Gillian.

'Where have you been? Luke's demented with worry. He thought you'd gone back to England!'

'*What*? Why should he think that?'

'It's obvious, surely?'

Suddenly it was, and Andrea was dismayed with herself for not realising how her long and unexpected absence from the hotel could be construed.

'Where's Luke now?' she asked.

'Gone to shower. He's been scouring the city for you and he came back exhausted. He went to the airport, the station, and goodness knows where else.'

With trembling fingers Andrea dialled his suite. 'I'm back,' she said the instant she heard his voice. 'I'm sorry you've been worried. It was very thoughtless of me.'

'Very.' His voice was so soft it was barely audible, and she knew the effort it was costing him to rein in his temper.

'Forgive me, Luke. I guess I wasn't thinking straight. But I wanted to be alone, and it was such a glorious day that I had to get out of the hotel.'

'Are you all right?'

'Yes. Yes, I really am.'

'Then so am I—now.'

Still feeling guilty, she said the first thing that came into her head. 'Fancy coming over for tea?'

There was a startled silence, then an explosive laugh. 'Thanks, but there isn't time. We should be leaving for the hall in about an hour.'

'Why so early? My dress will get creased!'

'Put on something comfortable and take your dress and make-up with you. All my artists do the same. You'll find it easier to relax in your dressing-room than at the hotel. I'll call you when the limousine arrives.'

'If you're leaving early, I'll follow on later,' Gillian said as Andrea replaced the receiver.

'Good idea. It's silly for you to hang around doing nothing.' Andrea glanced at her watch and hurried in to run a bath.

Soaking in the scented bubbles of Femme, she marvelled that she should be feeling so calm. Or was it the calm before the storm? Well, she would know soon enough!

Stepping from the bath, she reached for a bathrobe. As she went to wrap it round herself she saw her reflection in the mirror-lined wall facing her. Now that her hair was shorter at the sides, and with the dark fronds curling towards her cheeks, and her rounded limbs were sleek and shiny from the water, she had a gamine quality of innocence and sexual allure. No marks for guessing what Luke's reaction would be if he saw her now! She experienced a strong urge to be looked at with desire; to feel the sensuous pleasure of a man's hands on her body. But not any man—just a special one. Luke.

Pushing the thought aside, she slipped into cream silk panties and matching lace bra, then donned an over-sized cream cotton top and matching leggings. It made her look more waifish than ever, hinting at the grey-hound lines of the body it covered.

Forgoing make-up, other than mascara, without which she felt naked, she placed her evening dress in its plastic carrying cover, and was checking her cosmetic case when Gillian rushed in, a turquoise beaded shift in one hand and a slinky black crêpe in the other.

'Which do you think is more suitable for tonight?' she questioned.

Andrea looked at them, surprised to see that both bore the name of an expensive Rome boutique. 'Did you just buy them?'

'Yes, a couple of days ago.'

'Aren't you going overboard on evening dresses? You haven't yet worn the two Luke bought you at Hilary's.'

'So what? I still have my credit card, and Peter's financially responsible for me. After the way he be-haved I have every right to spend what I like.'

'From what you told me, I don't think he behaved badly,' Andrea couldn't help saying.

'You know nothing about it! He behaved like a swine and I never want to see him again.'

'But he wants to see *you*.' Andrea saw the opening and took it. Gillian was now well enough to know that Peter had followed her to London, and the least she could do was talk to him face to face. 'He arrived in England a few weeks ago.'

'Why didn't you tell me?'

'Dr Marshall thought you needed more time to come to yourself. But you're much better and——'

'Where's he staying? Have you seen him?' Gillian cut in.

'Yes. And he told me everything.'

'What do you mean?'

'About the baby, the car smash, and your breakdown afterwards.'

Gillian's face lost all its colour. 'It's lies! Lies!'

'It isn't. He gave Dr Marshall the name of your psychiatrist and the man confirmed everything.'

'They're *both* lying!'

'Don't be silly, darling, you know they're not. Peter loves you very much and he's desperately unhappy.' Andrea put her arm round Gillian in an attempt to placate her. 'Surely it's worth trying to patch up your differences?'

Angrily Gillian pushed her away. 'Stop interfering in my life. I know exactly why you want me to go back to him! It's because of Luke. You think that with me out of the way, you'll get him for yourself!'

'No! It's *your* happiness I'm concerned with.'

'Don't give me that! I've seen the way you look at him, the way you try to stop me going out with him. Well, you won't get him!' Gillian screamed. 'He loves me! He told me so.'

Her scream rose higher, the sound ricocheting round the room like a bullet. Andrea trembled with horror. Had the girl gone completely mad?

'Luke's only my manager,' she said loudly, trying to make herself heard. 'And he won't even be *that* when the tour's over. After my final concert in London I'll never see him again.'

'Not even when I'm married to him?'

Gillian's voice, normal again, sounded so confident that it was difficult not to believe her. And who was to say she was lying? All Andrea's doubts about Luke returned, and she faced the prospect of having him as a member of the family. Pain seared her, and it was all she could do to hide it.

'That—that would be different,' she said huskily. 'But—but are you sure you want to marry him? He let you down before and——'

'I don't care. I'm older now and more sophisticated about these things. Some men can't help being unfaithful, and Luke's one of them. But the love he has for me is different, and it means he'll never leave me. So stop trying to part us, *Annie*. You won't succeed.' She stormed to the door and, hand on the knob, swung round. 'Tell Peter to go back to Australia. Our marriage is over!'

The door slammed behind her and Andrea sank on to the bed. Her body felt icy cold and her hands were shaking. With the concert a few hours ahead it had been insane to choose this moment to confront Gillian. It would soon be time to leave for the hall, but instead of feeling serene, she was a mass of nerves.

An image of the auditorium flashed before her and, to her horror, was followed by the usual surge of panic. Oh, God! Her phobia hadn't gone. Leaning back on the pillows, she closed her eyes and breathed in and out deeply and slowly, trying to block off all thought.

The burr of the telephone jerked her back to the present, and she lifted it to hear Luke's voice.

'The car's waiting for us. Are you ready?'

'Yes.' She spoke calmly, relieved to find the panic had left her.

Gathering her evening dress and make-up bag, she went down to the lobby, deliberately not going in to say goodbye to Gillian in case it caused another upset.

Not catching sight of Luke, she went to the entrance. He wasn't there either, but a porter came over to take the things she was carrying, at the same time signalling to a chauffeur-driven limousine parked to one side of the entrance.

'I won't go in the car yet,' Andrea said. 'I'm waiting for Mr Luke.'

'I'm here,' he said behind her, and she swung round to see him.

He was heart-stoppingly handsome in evening clothes. As usual they were far from run of the mill: black and white check lining instead of the usual black satin, and thirties-style trousers with turn-ups.

'Forgive me if I don't come with you,' he said. 'I'm expecting a call from Paris. I'll join you later.'

'Fine.' Too conscious of what Gillian had said earlier to be at ease with him, Andrea avoided meeting his eyes and quickly climbed into the car.

Only as it pulled away did she glance back, discomfited to find that he had not turned to go but was watching her departure. Luckily another car drew up at the entrance, cutting him from sight, and she gave a deep sigh and closed her eyes, wishing that out of sight could also be out of mind.

When she opened her eyes again they were drawing to a stop outside the hall, and the manager was hurrying forward to open the car door and greet her, no doubt alerted to her arrival by Luke. He escorted her to her dressing-room, assured her she had only to ring for whatever she wanted, then tactfully left her.

The instant he did, she knew she couldn't bear sitting here by herself, and she jumped to her feet and headed for the auditorium.

As she pushed open the double doors she was struck by the vastness. It must seat over a thousand people. Two thousand eyes watching her, waiting to see if she would fail. Fear tightened her stomach muscles and she waited for the all too familiar surge of panic.

It didn't come. All she felt was the normal fear any artist might have in similar circumstances.

Impulsively she ran out of the auditorium and into the street. On the opposite side of the road a small church nestled between two office blocks, and without conscious thought she found herself pushing open the heavy wooden door and walking down the dim central aisle. Halfway along she stopped and knelt in a pew, then, head bent, hands clasped, she gave thanks for her new-found peace.

It wasn't until she became aware of someone sliding into the pew beside her that she opened her eyes and saw Luke.

'What are *you* doing here?' she whispered.

'I came to find you.'

She rose and they left the church together. 'How did you know where I was?'

'I had a hunch.'

In silence they returned to the concert hall and her dressing-room. To her surprise it was filled with flowers: bouquets set in vases and baskets of towering blooms, as well as masses of cards and telegrams from well-wishers. Tears sprang to her eyes and she fumbled for a handkerchief.

'Don't get into a state again,' Luke said. 'It's important you stay calm.'

'I'm perfectly calm.' Something in his expression alerted her and she frowned. 'What do you mean by *again*?'

'Nothing. I merely want you to relax.'

'But you used the word "again" and I'd like to know why.'

'There was no reason. It was a slip of the tongue.' He went to the door. 'I suggest you rest for an hour. I'll come back later to——'

'You weren't delayed by a call from Paris,' Andrea said with a flash of insight. 'It was Gillian who called you, wasn't it?'

'Yes,' Luke admitted slowly. 'She telephoned me when you left the suite and said she had to see me. She said you'd been hysterical and she blamed herself for it.'

'Really?' Waiting to hear more before she said anything, Andrea pretended to fuss with some greeting cards on the dressing-table.

'I know you have a problem performing in front of an audience,' Luke said gently, coming to stand behind her. 'But it's wrong to go on blaming Gillian for it. She's upset enough about her divorce without you adding to her stress. The poor girl's felt guilty about you for years. But it isn't her fault you've let a silly incident build into——'

'Silly incident!' Andrea cut in stormily. 'I'd hardly call it that. It gave me nightmares for years.'

'That was probably your way of getting your parents' sympathy. You felt they believed Gillian's side of the story and——'

'She never told them. They didn't *know* what happened. That was the trouble. If I could have talked to them about it . . . But she swore me to secrecy.'

Luke frowned. 'I don't understand.'

'Obviously. What did she actually tell you?'

'That you went with her to the park to go boating, but changed your mind and ran off to the playground. She ran after you but apparently you got lost, and when she found you, a gang of little boys were teasing you and she chased them away.'

She was disgusted to find that Gillian was as manipulative as ever, and Andrea's loyalty to her died. 'Little boys of sixteen,' she said quietly, and in the same tones, recounted what had really taken place.

'Two women, two different stories,' she concluded. 'It's your choice.'

'Where you are concerned, I have no choice,' Luke said huskily. 'I would always believe *you*. But why didn't you tell me all this when you first came to see me to discuss the tour? If you had, I'd have cancelled it.'

'I'm glad you didn't. Coming to Rome has been a catalyst for me.' Happily she recounted her visit to the Ponte Sisto and all that had resulted from it. 'I'm free of the past, Luke. It's the most wonderful thing that's happened to me.'

'I still can't figure out why Gillian lied,' he muttered.

'I guess she was afraid that if you knew the truth, it would affect your—your love for her.'

'I do *not* love her!' he practically roared. 'Though if she's lied to me about *you*, lord knows what lies she told you about *me*. So I'll set the record straight once more and remind you the only reason I saw her was that it meant I could see *you*. You made it plain you despised me, and I figured if I could infiltrate into your life you might lose your prejudice against me. I love you, Andrea. I was fond of you when you were a spotty teenager, but the moment you walked into my office, a mature and beautiful woman, I knew I wanted to spend the rest of my days with you.'

'I can't see you being faithful to one woman,' she said lightly. 'That isn't the Luke Kane whose antics have filled yards of tabloid space.'

His chiselled features narrowed, giving her an inkling of how he would look in his sixties. Just as devastating as he did now! she acknowledged.

'For the record, I wasn't unfaithful to your sister, despite what she said. But I was eternally grateful she ran off with someone else, because a few months after she did, I realised what a lucky escape I'd had! As for my reputation ... Sure, I played the field, but no more than any man my age, and definitely not to the extent that was reported in the Press.' A long-fingered hand raked back the lock of black hair that had fallen across his forehead. 'Since the day I fell in love with you I haven't touched another woman. I know you aren't interested in a permanent relationship, but if you'd let me share part of your life...' His voice grew ragged. 'I'll take whatever you give me, Andrea, and in time you may even decide——' He broke off and shook his head. 'No, I won't pressure you. I promise.'

'You'll never ask me to marry you?'

'Never.'

She gazed deep into his eyes. 'Then I'll have to ask *you.*'

For infinite seconds he stared at her, then with a deep-throated groan he gathered her close.

'That note you left me after we spent the night together,' he said against her skin. 'Why did——?'

'I thought you were only interested in an affair and I didn't want you to know what I really felt.'

'What *do* you feel?' he asked thickly.

'That you are everything to me; my reason for waking up in the morning.'

'And for going to bed at night too, I hope?'

'That too!' she smiled, the rest of her words stifled by his mouth coming down on hers.

She was aware of the heavy thudding of his heart as her nearness stirred him to desire and, murmuring her name, he softly kissed her brow, her eyelids, her temple, then let his lips find hers again. Only then did the softness vanish and the pressure increase, until her body was bent back and his arms alone prevented her falling.

'You're mine,' he said. 'Mine forever.'

'I've longed for you to say that!'

Twining her arms round his neck, she strained closer to him. The tip of his tongue rubbed the pearly edge of her teeth, and he uttered a throaty sound as his hands crept beneath the hem of her top and caressed the smooth skin of her back, then came round to cup the fullness of her breasts. Her body grew warm with her need of him, but as his hands moved lower still she caught them and pushed them away.

'Darling, no! I have to go on stage soon and I must get ready.'

'Damn! I'd forgotten the concert! That's the effect you have on me.' Reluctantly he released her and strode to the door. 'I'll be back as soon as you've changed.'

'There's no need for you to go.' Her eyes crinkled at him provocatively. 'It's late in the day for me to play the blushing virgin!'

Pulling off her top and leggings, she revealed a wisp of lacy bra and panties. Quickly she removed the bra, and as her breasts swung free Luke involuntarily reached for her.

'No touching,' she warned, grabbing her evening dress and holding it defensively in front of her.

'It will be safer for both of us if I leave you alone to get changed,' he said whimsically. 'I'll be back in half an hour.'

The door closed behind him, and shakily she sat down at the dressing-table and opened her make-up box. Who would have thought that in the space of a quarter of an hour her entire life would change? Yet miraculously it had, and her future was as bright and rosy as the lipstick in her hand.

She was fastening the bodice of her dramatic scarlet and orange dress when Luke returned.

'I've never seen you more glowing. You'll make the spotlights look dim!'

Taking her hand, he led her along the stone-floored passage towards the stage. She walked as if under heavy sedation. The people they passed seemed miles away, and she was oblivious of the backstage excitement. As they reached the wings, Luke released her and lowered his head to look deep into her eyes.

'I know you want to give of your best, my darling. But if you have any——' he hesitated '—any problems, just remember that whatever happens I am here, waiting for you.'

Barely conscious of what he had said, she stepped boldly forward. There was a sudden hush as her slender figure appeared on stage, then the auditorium was filled with applause that did not die down until she had seated herself at the piano.

For a few seconds there was complete silence. As if in slow motion the conductor lifted his baton and Andrea raised her hands above the keyboard, then brought them down swiftly and assuredly for the first chords of Beethoven's 'Emperor' Concerto.

CHAPTER FIFTEEN

LOOKING back later, Andrea remembered little about her performance. One thing she did know was that she was playing with a greater depth of emotion, and she finally understood what Luke had meant when he had said she would not reach her peak as a pianist until she had fallen in love.

The second half of the concert remained as much of a dream as the first. At one point she had a moment of panic. Then the words he had said to her before she came on stage came vividly to mind, and she was filled with an inner peace that restored her equilibrium.

It was not until her hands lifted after the final chords of the Rachmaninov Piano Concerto that she returned to the present. The lights came fully on and there was a deathly hush. Then the audience rose as one and with cries of '*Magnifico!*' gave her a standing ovation. Bouquets of flowers were presented to her by attendants, and roses and carnations were flung from the stalls and upper circle to lie in a shower of pink and scarlet at her feet. The clapping and cheering increased in intensity as she walked off the stage and she stared dumbly at Luke, who gathered her into his arms and shook his head.

'No, darling, I won't let you give an encore,' he answered her unspoken question. 'You were sensational, and you've given enough of yourself tonight.'

Grateful for his understanding, she let him lead her to her dressing-room, where she collapsed into a chair. Later she would feel triumph, but for the moment she was too exhausted to feel anything.

'Drink this,' he ordered, bending over her with a glass of brandy.

'I can't bear the taste.'

'Think of it as medicine,' he grinned, and she downed it at a gulp, shuddering as she did. Warmth enveloped her immediately and she visibly unwound.

'The concert went well, didn't it?' she questioned.

'It was faultless. From first glittering chord to last, you played as if you were inspired.'

'I think I was.' She longed to add 'by you', but found herself strangely shy.

'I'll take you back to the hotel soon,' he said. 'The Press are clamouring to talk to you, but I instructed the manager not to let them backstage.'

'Turning away publicity? That's not like you!'

'You'll get it without having to see them tonight.' He went to the door.

'Where are you going?' she called, inexplicably afraid.

'To see if there's another way we can get out.'

As he stepped into the passage, she heard Gillian's voice, then the door burst open and the girl breezed in.

'I've been trying to see you for the last five minutes,' she exclaimed. 'But the corridor's jammed with bossy officials. I told them I was your sister but they didn't believe me.'

'They probably thought you were a reporter.'

Gillian, cover-girl-pretty in her turquoise shift, seemed to have forgotten their acrimonious parting, nor did she appear to realise Luke might have recounted the web of lies she had spun. Andrea marvelled that her stepsister was so confident of her power over him.

'You were fantastic!' Gillian gushed, taking a chair and helping herself to some nuts from a dish on a side-table. 'Any champagne?'

'No. There's some brandy, though.'

'Ugh!'

'I said the same, but Luke insisted I have some, and it certainly helped calm me.'

Colour stained the older girl's face. 'It was my fault, wasn't it? That you were in a state, I mean. I behaved like an idiot and I owe you an apology.'

Andrea found it difficult to be forgiving. 'They say one shouldn't· interfere between a husband and wife, and you certainly proved it,' she murmured.

'It wasn't your comments about Peter that annoyed me,' came the surprising answer. 'It's what you said about Luke. But when I thought it over afterwards I understood why. You've had a crush on him since you were a kid, so it's not surprising you're jealous.'

'I've no cause to be jealous.' Andrea decided to put paid to her stepsister's illusions; the sooner she learned the truth, the better. 'Luke loves me. He told me just before the concert.'

Gillian giggled. 'He's even more unscrupulous than I thought.'

'If you're implying he doesn't mean it . . .'

'I'm not *implying*, Annie, I'm *telling* you. He may fancy going to bed with you, but he's no more in love with you than with any of his other women! His declaration of love this evening was the best way he knew of giving you the confidence not to run off stage. He was scared stiff you would, and he lied to protect his interests.'

It was a logical assumption, Andrea knew, and though she dismissed it verbally, it left a niggle of doubt in its wake.

'You never give up, do you, Gillian? But if Luke is as duplicitous as you say, how can *you* trust him?'

'Because I know him warts and all. That's why I'm the only woman with whom he's totally at ease. With me, he doesn't have to pretend.'

'But *you* have to pretend.'

'What do you mean?'

'Why else did you tell him a load of lies about what happened in the park when I was a child?'

For the first time Gillian was disconcerted. 'He told you?'

'Everything. You can't be as certain of his love as you say or you'd have been honest with him.'

'I didn't want him thinking badly of me, so I doctored the truth a little.'

'A little? You completely distorted it!'

Before Gillian could reply, Luke came in, and silently Andrea watched him, fighting the urge to rush into his arms. Please God, let Gillian be wrong, she prayed, and waited for him to come closer. But he remained by the door.

'We can leave by the staff exit,' he informed them. 'I've had a scout around and there's no one there. But we must hurry.'

Like three conspirators, they scurried down the stone-floored passage to the narrow steel door that opened into a side-alley, at the bottom of which waited their chauffeured limousine. Only as they passed the concert hall, where crowds of people were milling around, did Andrea breathe a sigh of relief. Much as she enjoyed the appreciation of her fans, tonight she was in no mood to respond to it.

'Do you think you can cope with the reception I've arranged at the hotel?' Luke asked her.

'Reception?' Dismayed, she regarded him.

'There won't be any journalists there, just some VIPs from the music world. You needn't stay long.'

'I'll stay as long as you think necessary,' she replied, and felt a surge of joy as his hand grasped hers and caressed the softness of her palm.

The car approached the hotel entrance and they saw that it was thronged with photographers.

Luke swore under his breath. 'They must have taken a shorter route than us.'

'I might as well see them and get it over with,' she said. 'Then at least I can relax tomorrow.'

The car drew to a halt and, as she stepped out, flashlights half blinded her. Questions were thrown thick and fast. Did her success tonight mean she was going to do more tours? Had she been scared of running off the stage as she had done years ago? And would she now come clean and give the real reason why she had refused to give concert performances until now?

She answered each probe as best she could, aware of Luke standing protectively at her side, and her step-sister basking in reflected glory. But eventually she could take no more and, sensing it, he peremptorily ushered her into the safety of the hotel, leaving Gillian to enjoy their undivided attention.

'I'd like to go to my room to freshen up,' she said as casually as she could. 'Care to keep me company?'

'There's nothing I'd like more, but I have to check that everything's been laid on in the private dining-room.'

She forced a smile. 'I'll join you there, then.'

She was on the brink of tears as she entered her suite, but refusing to give vent to them she went into the bathroom to touch up her make-up. The strain of the concert—or perhaps it was what she had learned after it—had brought a hectic flush to her cheeks, and this, coupled with the vibrant pink silk of her halter top and the glowing orange silk wrap-around skirt, gave her an exotic magnetism which would attract far more men than her stepsister's chocolate-box prettiness. Yet this didn't mean that Luke would find her more alluring. Indeed, if Gillian was not to be discounted, the pull of the past was stronger for him.

She was mulling this over as she entered the private room on the fifth floor. Luke was instantly by her side and introduced her to her guests. There was the chief shareholder of a major record company, a newspaper mogul, the owner of a chain of theatres, and the president of an important American television network. She noticed they all treated him as a personal friend, not a business acquaintance, and for the first time realised how great his influence was and how far he had come in his career. No wonder Abraham had had no doubts when handing over the agency to him!

The evening passed in a whirl. She must have said and done the right things, for whenever she looked Luke's way he nodded approvingly, but by the time coffee was served she was drained to the point of collapse.

'How long until we can get away?' she murmured as he sauntered over to her.

'Not for at least an hour. We're going to the Starlight Room to dance. But you may leave if you wish. You've more than done your duty.'

'I was hoping we——' She stopped as an elegant
woman in her late thirties—whom he had earlier introduced as Carlotta, Contessa Fragiani, who had inher-
ited her late husband's newspaper empire—joined
them, and watching her flirt with him, Andrea was be-
set by jealousy. Even if he really did love her, was he
capable of being faithful?

Hiding her despondency under a bright veneer, she
followed everyone to the nightclub, where Luke had reserved a large table, and as soon as they were all seated
around it, he asked her to dance.

Instantly her despondency disappeared, and she followed him on to the crowded floor, where a Latin
American trio were playing a rumba at a bearable level.
For a brief instant he stood next to her without touching her, but there was such intimacy in his glance that
she trembled; then he drew her close and she gave herself up to his arms and the music.

It was no surprise to find that he was an easy, effort-
less dancer: light on his feet, his hold gentle yet firmly
guiding her. A man of control who was used to control. She trembled, recognising how vulnerable her love
made her.

'When I feel you tremble like this I want to make love
to you,' he whispered into her ear.

'I feel the same.'

He rested his cheek on hers and she felt the faint
brush of stubble rub her skin, intensely masculine, intensely erotic. Her body grew warm and she was aware
of the softness of her breasts pressing into the hardness
of his chest, and the steel-like muscles of his thighs as
they moved against hers.

They danced in silence, their bodies speaking for
them, and they were still mute when the music momen-

tarily stopped and they found themselves alongside the contessa and her escort, an elderly grey-haired man.

As the trio resumed playing, the woman placed a silver-tipped hand on Luke's sleeve. 'I'm anxious to have your advice about the music magazine I'm launching in the spring.' Almond-shaped eyes turned to Andrea. 'I hope you won't mind changing partners?'

'Not at all.' She stepped towards the grey-haired man and, over his shoulder, watched Luke's arms wrap themselves round Carlotta's reed-slim body. From the way the woman nestled close to him, it was clear that her need of advice was an excuse to dance with him; she might even be launching the magazine in the hope of its bringing her legitimately into his orbit. The things women did for love! No, not love, she amended, studying the hard profile and blatantly provocative mouth—just sex.

As soon as decency allowed, Andrea pleaded tiredness and her partner led her back to the table. He was interesting to talk to, but it was an effort not to let her attention wander to the man and woman on the dancefloor, who were so intent upon one another that they were hardly dancing: their bodies close and moving imperceptibly.

The music continued unabated, one number merging into another, but Luke gave no sign of wishing to leave the floor. On the contrary, he had changed partners and was dancing with Gillian as intimately as he had with Carlotta.

Jealousy welled up so strongly in Andrea that it propelled her to her feet. 'If you'll excuse me, I'm very tired,' she announced to the rest of the table.

With their regrets echoing in her ears she went into the satin-draped foyer and rang for the lift.

'Darling, wait!' Luke said behind her, and she turned to see him coming towards her. 'Sorry I wasn't able to dance with you again, but Gillian grabbed me as I was leaving the floor and I couldn't escape her. She still won't believe that what I felt for her in my early twenties no longer exists.'

'Maybe you should try harder.'

'I would if her marriage weren't in trouble, but I don't want to hurt her while she's down. I'm hoping that when she sees *our* relationship she'll leave me alone.' His grey eyes darkened as he caught her hand and lifted it to his mouth to press a kiss in her soft palm. 'And that's what I'd like for us—to be alone. God! I wish I weren't hosting this party, but I have to stay till it shows signs of breaking up. So, my darling,' he went on as the lift door opened and he gently pushed her inside, 'dream well, and tomorrow night I'll turn those dreams into reality!'

The door closed and she pressed the indicator for her floor. Luke's parting words had reassured her, making it easy to dismiss everything Gillian had said as the ranting of an envious woman.

Walking down the corridor to her suite, she was conscious how quiet it was. Not to be wondered at when carpet underfoot deadened her steps, and heavy bedroom doors, leather-panelled, muffled any sounds that might have come from within. Why, one could be attacked without anyone hearing!

Hardly had the thought entered her head when she became conscious of a padding sound behind her. She quickened her pace and the padding sound quickened. Her heart began to pound and her hands grew clammy but she couldn't bring herself to look round. Instead she broke into a run, terror gripping her as the padding became the distinct sound of feet running fast, gaining ground on her. Even if she reached her room ahead of her pursuer, he would catch her before she got her key into the lock. She opened her mouth to scream, but the sound was choked off as hard fingers gripped her shoulders and pulled her to a stop.

'Stop running!' a hard male voice ordered. 'I'm going to talk to you whether you like it or not.'

Dumbstruck, she found herself facing Peter. 'What are *you* doing here? When did you arrive?'

'Earlier this evening. I've come to see my wife.'

'But you agreed to wait until——'

'I didn't so much agree as was bludgeoned into it,' he cut in. 'But I'm sick of waiting and I intend talking to her whatever you say.'

'You'll lose her if you do,' Andrea said bluntly. Beyond his shoulder she saw an elderly woman emerge from a lift and, worried that the next time it might disgorge Gillian—and heaven alone knew how she would react at sight of her husband—she said hurriedly, 'We can't stand here in case you're seen. Gillian thinks I told you to go back to Australia. Tell me where you're staying and I'll talk to you tomorrow.'

'I'm staying here and you'll talk to me tonight.'

Catching her arm in a bruising hold, he pulled her along the corridor and, avoiding the lift, pushed open a door marked 'stairway,' showing that, angry though he was, he had taken note of her comment about his not being seen.

'My room's on the floor above you,' he explained, and said nothing further until they were inside it. 'Now then, why do you think I'll lose her if I confront her?'

'Because she's still convinced Luke will marry her.'

'Oh, God!'

'I'm sorry, Peter.' Sympathetically she touched his arm, distressed at how thin and haggard he had become since they had last met. 'Give it a few more days. I may be able to talk some sense into her.'

'How?'

She hesitated, unwilling to admit that it depended on the way Luke acted towards her. 'Trust me, Peter. You've been patient so long, a little longer won't matter. We're leaving for Paris tomorrow—we'll be at the Ritz—and I suggest you join us at the end of the week.'

He sighed heavily. 'From what Gillian told me about Luke's reputation, I bet they've already gone to bed together. A man who was unfaithful to his fiancée wouldn't have any scruples seducing a woman who's run away from her husband.'

Hearing Peter voice thoughts she had never dared say aloud gave them greater credence, and she felt the blood drain from her head.

'You OK, Andrea? You're pale as a ghost.'

'I'm a little dizzy. I've had a hectic day.'

'And I've added to it.' Firmly yet gently he propelled her into a nearby armchair and pushed her head down between her legs. 'Stay there till you feel better.'

It was several moments before she did, and when she raised her head he was holding out a balloon glass of brandy. Gratefully she sipped it, disliking the taste but glad of the warmth that began permeating her limbs.

'I've been a thoughtless oaf,' he grunted. 'You must have been drained after the concert, and there was I, scaring you to death, chasing you down the corridor, and then dragging you here and—heck, I don't know what got into me.'

'Love and desperation,' she said drily. 'It's a feeling I understand.'

'You?'

Stifling a yawn, which also stifled his next question, she was glad to see, she rose. In the mirror in the little vestibule she was taken aback to see how dishevelled her hair was—putting her head between her knees had made her look as though she had been dragged backwards through a hedge—but she was too tired to do more than push it away from her forehead.

'Don't worry, you look fine,' Peter assured her, opening the door for her and stepping out. 'I'll see you back to your suite.'

'Oh, no, you won't!' Only as she saw his slight smile did she realise he was teasing. 'And when you get to the Ritz, keep out of sight.'

'Not for much longer, I hope.'

'So do I.' Lightly touching his arm, she sped away.

The suite was still empty when she returned to it, and she wandered on to the balcony and stared at the star-spattered sky, aware of the immensity of the universe and the smallness of Man. Yet it did nothing to diminish the desolation she felt. Luke's track record, which Gillian and Peter had brought firmly to the forefront of her mind, did not augur well for his ability to sustain a faithful relationship. She had known it weeks ago, when she had walked out on him the night they had made love, but this evening, before the concert, she had allowed herself to forget it, and she prayed that it wasn't going to be a decision she would regret.

CHAPTER SIXTEEN

ANDREA awoke at nine o'clock to find sunlight streaming through the curtains. She lay for a while, mulling over the events of yesterday, culminating in her meeting with Peter. From beginning to end it had been a day of stress—but with one lasting consolation: she had finally played before a live audience without breaking down, and she had played magnificently.

Pushing aside the bedclothes, she ran a bath, then had a leisurely breakfast at a table set out by the window, and read the reviews of her concert. They were unanimous in their praise of her playing, though in the popular Press the comments on her high-fashion profile featured more prominently than her performance! The consensus was that were she ever to change her profession, she could grace a designer's catwalk as easily as the concert platform. Luke was given full credit for her metamorphosis, and there were several pictures of her before he had played Svengali. Studying them, she had to concede that she preferred her new image, even if she was not yet completely comfortable with it.

At ten-thirty Luke had not telephoned, and his silence weighed heavily on her. But she refused to call and see where he was in case he thought she was checking on him, and to quell her anxiety she began packing.

When she had finished, there was still no sign of him, and Carlotta Fragiani's face floated into the room like a mirage. Had Luke spent the night with her?

'I'm getting paranoid,' Andrea muttered aloud. If her trust in him was so frail, what sort of future could they have? Except that he hadn't mentioned their future nor made reference to any kind of commitment. Not that there'd been time. Since his saying how he felt about her, they had hardly had a moment alone.

Andrea stared out of the window. The blue sky had disappeared and, like her mood, the sky was grey and gloomy. There was a tap on the door and she ran across to open it, her mood lifting as she saw Luke standing there, arms filled with bouquets of flowers.

'There are more downstairs, but I instructed the hall porter to send them to the local hospital.'

'Those could have gone too,' she said, eyeing the scented roses and carnations.

'You might prefer to give them to the maids on this floor.'

It was a nice thought, and she couldn't help wondering if his declaration of love last night had been equally as well thought out. Stop it, she admonished herself, and gave him a brilliant smile. But he had turned to set the flowers on a side-table, and did not see it.

He was casually dressed in jeans and a heavy ribbed blue cotton sweater that gave clear indication of the smoothly flexing muscles of his chest. But there were lines of tiredness fanning out from his eyes, and she longed to gather him close.

'What time did the party break up?' she said instead.

'It didn't. Carlotta insisted we go back to her palazzo to see the dummy of her new magazine.'

'Is it any good?'

'No better than any other. But if it goes down the tubes she'll write it off as a tax loss and embark on another project.'

'I think *you* are her ultimate project.'

A shrug was his only answer, and when he spoke it was to change the subject. 'I had all the newspapers sent up to you. Have you read the reviews?'

'Even before I looked at my horoscope!' she smiled, but no answering humour lightened his face, and she went on, 'They were great, weren't they? And flattering to you too.'

'Oh?' An eyebrow rose.

'Yes. One of the tabloids said you'd make a great fashion consultant!'

This time he did smile. 'I hope all those marvellous clothes I chose for you are packed? We leave for the airport at noon.'

'Then I'd better wake Gillian or she'll never be ready.'

'By the way, I won't be staying with you in Paris,' Luke said as she crossed to the bedroom door. 'I have to be in London tonight.'

'When will you come back?'

'I won't. Alan Bradly will be taking my place for the remainder of your tour.'

Speechlessly she stared at him. Alan had taken care of her some weeks ago when Luke, furious with her for walking out on him the night they had made love, had deputed him to take care of her. Now he was doing the same, but this time she had no idea why.

'Why bother coming to Paris at all?' she said. 'It would be less hassle for you to fly direct to London.'

'I agree. But there are several practical details I want to sort out myself.' He rubbed the side of his face.

'When you choose your new manager make sure he's good at attending to minutiae. It's essential he keep your mind worry-free so you can concentrate on your playing.'

Not sure she had heard him correctly, Andrea shook her head. After what had happened between them in the dressing-room last night, how could he possibly believe she still wanted someone else to manage her career?

'I—I intend staying with *your* agency,' she stammered. 'After last night, surely you realise that?'

'Why should I? An artist must do what they feel is best for their career, irrespective of personal feelings.'

'Do you want me to find another manager?' Flinging pride to the wind, she ran over to him. 'Didn't you mean what you said to me? Was Gillian right?'

'As I've no idea what she said——'

'That you only told me you loved me because you wanted to give me confidence before the concert.'

'Well, it did the trick, didn't it?'

Andrea stared at him incredulously. She had always known he was single-minded, but had never imagined he would deliberately play on her emotions to obtain what he wanted. True, what he had wanted was her success, but to achieve it in such a manner...

'It was a disgusting thing to do,' she burst out.

'Give it a few days and you won't think the same. It wouldn't work for us, you know. Old feelings don't necessarily die just because you bury them.'

'I don't follow you.'

'For years you've regarded me as a womaniser, and those feelings will resurface each time you see me with an attractive female. But my world is full of attractive women—just as yours is full of good-looking men.' His mouth tightened into a thin line. 'I suggest we leave it at that and go our separate ways.'

'Good morning, you two,' Gillian called, emerging from her room. 'Am I breaking up a private conversation?'

'Not at all,' Luke smiled. 'Though we'll have to break the speed limit if you don't get on with your packing. We're leaving at noon.'

With a yelp, Gillian disappeared and Andrea did the same, her control only lasting till she was in the safety of her bathroom and could burst into tears without being heard. Luke had broken her heart but she wasn't going to let him know it. Never.

Throughout the drive to the airport and flight to Paris, she moved and talked like an automaton. As long as she kept her mind blank she could manage, but once she started thinking...

'Are you all right?' Luke asked at one stage of their trip. 'You're very quiet.'

'I'm fine,' she lied, and he took her at her word and resumed reading the contract he had extracted from his briefcase.

They were met by the Press at Charles de Gaulle Airport, and watching the skilful way Luke handled them, she wondered how she would ever replace him. Realising her complete turn-around in attitude compared with a couple of weeks ago, she had to restrain a bitter smile. How people changed!

Entering her suite at the Ritz, she found it overflowing with flowers and goodwill messages from most of the people she had met in Rome. She was so touched by their kindness that her composure cracked, and she couldn't stop the tears flowing.

'Annie, what's wrong?' Gillian rushed over to her.

Andrea responded by burying her head in her hands and crying all the harder.

'It's to do with Luke, isn't it?' Gillian guessed shrewdly.

'Yes, but I don't want to discuss it. Leave me alone.'

'So you can wallow in your misery? That's the worst thing to do, and believe me, I should know.'

Surprised at this confidence, Andrea was sufficiently roused from her feelings to think of Peter, waiting miserably in a Rome hotel. Perhaps now was a good time to confess that he was coming to Paris in a few days. Without any preamble she did and, as expected, Gillian was livid.

'I told you in Rome I didn't want to see him!' she stormed. 'You had no right encouraging him to follow me here. Call him this minute and tell him he's wasting his time and should go home.'

'Why are you scared of meeting him?'

As Gillian went to reply, the telephone rang and she answered it, her eyes widening in horror as she recognised the voice at the other end. 'It's Peter!' she mouthed, practically throwing the receiver in Andrea's direction. 'He's already here—at Reception! *You* talk to him.'

'No!' Andrea jumped to her feet and hurried into her bedroom. She was through interfering in Gillian's life. Her stepsister was well enough to handle things herself.

She was pacing the carpet, wondering if she had done the right thing, when Gillian tapped on the door and came in. A sheen of sweat glistened on her forehead, but when she spoke she sounded composed.

'Peter says to tell you he's sorry but he couldn't wait in Rome. He caught the plane after ours. He's in the lobby and wants me to come down.'

'Wouldn't you rather talk to him up here on your own? I'll go out for a stroll.'

'No. It's better if I meet him with people around. Otherwise it might get too emotional.' She smoothed her hair. 'I'll be back soon. What I have to say to him won't take long.'

Alone, Andrea unpacked, then took a shower. How stupid she had been over Luke! Knowing his declaration of love had merely been an expedient one was almost too much to bear. Thank goodness she hadn't gone to bed with him again. The humiliation of being dumped afterwards would have been the ultimate degradation. Wrapping herself in a bathcoat, she opened her wardrobe and riffled through her dresses until she found a brightly patterned cotton. Even if she felt miserable, she could at least look bright.

Returning to the sitting-room, she sank into a well cushioned blue silk armchair and studied her schedule for the rest of the week. She was giving three concerts in Paris and would have to devote each morning to a practice session. A strange exhilaration filled her, and she knew it was due to the knowledge that she need never fear her playing would let her down. Her belief in Luke's love had served as a prop to get her on stage; a bolster to her new-found confidence, not the prime cause. *That* had come from her own inner strength.

A key turned in the lock and she tensed as Gillian came in. But sight of her radiant face, and that of Peter's behind her, brought her happily to her feet.

'Waiting in Europe paid off,' he grinned. 'I've got my wife back!'

'I can't explain it,' Gillian murmured in a shaky voice. 'When I went down I was hell-bent on telling him to get lost. But as soon as I saw him I knew I loved him

as much as ever. When I think of the horrible things I
said about him . . .'

'Forget it,' Peter murmured. 'I'm sure Andrea un-
derstands.'

'If it hadn't been for her we'd never have got together again,' Gillian cried, rushing forward to clasp her
close. 'I know I haven't been easy to have around, and
I must have driven you crazy the way I acted with Luke.
I lied about still being in love with him. I did it to make
myself feel good.'

'I thought so,' Andrea said as calmly as she could.
'Now why don't you forget the past and concentrate on
the future? And for starters, I suggest the two of you go
off and enjoy yourselves. Paris is a magical city for
lovers.'

Gillian swung round to Peter. 'Where to first?
Versailles, exploring the Left Bank, or the art galleries?'

'The galleries every time,' came the prompt reply.
'Let's start by looking at the etchings in my room!'

Blushing, Gillian clasped his hand and together they
went out, leaving Andrea blinking away the tears. At
least *something* nice had occurred today. Determined to
follow the advice she had just given—to forget the past
and concentrate on the future—she sat down and studied her schedule again.

She was still on the first page when Luke rang to say
his deputy had arrived from London and he'd like to
bring him over. Schooling herself to face Luke, she
greeted him at the door, glancing briefly at him before
smiling at Alan Bradly. He was as tow-haired and
tanned as she remembered, and he still reminded her of
a Californian lifeguard!

'Long time no see,' he grinned, 'but I've read every one of your rave reviews.'

'Flattery will get you everything,' she said.

'May I begin with a drink?'

'Of course.' She glanced at Luke but he shook his head.

'Not for me, thanks. I have to be on my way.' His brief smile encompassed her and Alan. 'You know where to reach me in an emergency. But I'm sure it won't be necessary.'

Lightly he kissed her on both cheeks, the gesture of an entrepreneur to one of his leading stars.

'I'm delighted to be taking care of you,' Alan said. 'I must say, I was surprised when Luke asked me to come here. He's been very proprietorial about you.'

'He's obviously found someone else more important,' she murmured easily.

'Well, he's taking over an agency in the States, so I guess he wants to keep a close eye on it till all the problems are ironed out. But I have orders to fax him after each of your concerts, and send him the tapes of your radio and television interviews, so he's keeping tabs on you just the same.'

Business expedience, Andrea thought bitterly; it had nothing to do with caring.

In the weeks that followed she was to think this many times, especially at night when, the applause and interviews over, she lay in bed and considered how to live the rest of her life. She didn't want music to become the be-all and end-all of her existence. She wanted a loving husband and children, and though she did not envisage loving any other man with the same depth she had loved Luke, she was adult enough to concede that she would eventually compromise.

Her concerts in Paris were a great success, and from there she travelled to Madrid, Vienna and Brussels. Gillian and Peter accompanied her to Spain, but then decided to return to London, where they would remain until her return.

It was a relief when they left, for sight of Gillian was a constant reminder of Luke; indeed whenever Gillian had tried to talk about him, Andrea had changed the subject.

On the last concert of her tour Andrea had an unexpected attack of stage fright, but the instant her hands touched the keyboard she regained control of her nerves and played with unsurpassed brilliance.

'I've never heard the Grieg concerto played better,' Alan greeted her as she came into the wings. 'I hope you'll play it for your command performance.'

'My what?'

'Hasn't Luke phoned you with the news? You've been asked to appear at a concert in aid of one of the Queen's favourite charities, and she'll be attending.'

Andrea was overwhelmed. She had dreamed of something like this, but given her previous fears, had never envisaged it happening.

But what was Luke doing, arranging it for her? Hadn't he made it clear that he expected her to find another manager? Still, if he'd been approached by the Palace, he could hardly turn it down, any more than she could. And if this was going to be her last performance with Kane Enterprises, then at least she would go out on a high note!

Lying in bed on the last night of her stay in Brussels, Andrea was sick with despair at the thought of returning to London and seeing Luke again. It would take a long time to get over her love for him. But no pain lasted forever, and one day she would hopefully be able to think about him without this dreadful sense of loss. She gave a bitter smile. How could you lose someone you'd never possessed? She doubted whether any woman would ever possess Luke.

She glanced down at her hands, the hands that had brought her fame and fortune, and flexed her fingers. They were ringless, and with a terribly certainty she knew that unless she exorcised Luke from her system, they would always remain so.

CHAPTER SEVENTEEN

ANDREA'S hope, faint yet persistent, that Luke would contact her on her return to London and say he hadn't meant a word of what he had said in Paris, and that he still loved her, died a painful death when, after being home nearly two months, she still hadn't heard from him.

True, he had sent her a message via Alan after her triumph in Brussels, and a magnificent basket of flowers had been awaiting her on her return home, but the card that accompanied it had been cool to the point of coldness.

Yet for the first few weeks she couldn't quench the hope that he would want to see her again, and every time the telephone rang or someone came to the front door, she momentarily tensed in case it was him.

It wasn't until she was glancing at a magazine one morning at her hairdresser's and saw a series of pictures of him at the races, at the opera, and half a dozen other events—accompanied on each occasion by Amalia Nichols, a blonde young violinist who had joined his agency the same time as herself and who was now—according to the writer of the article—his constant companion and good friend, that she finally faced the fact that her silly pipe-dreams had gone up in smoke.

'I won't waste my life pining for him,' she said aloud, hoping that hearing her words would lend them greater weight. 'I'm going to date other men. Luke isn't the only one in the world. There must be thousands like him!'

Trouble was, there weren't; leastwise not for her.

She was certain he would personally handle all the arrangements for her command performance, and dreaded the prospect of meeting him, bolstering her courage by telling herself that for most of their association she had successfully hidden her feelings for him, so it shouldn't be too much of a problem to do the same again.

None the less she was relieved when Alan rang to say he'd been deputed to supervise the arrangements for the concert, and hoped she wasn't too disappointed.

'What a silly question,' she chided. 'You're so good that Luke should look to his laurels.'

'You wouldn't like to put that in writing, would you?'

'Will it do any good?'

'Not really,' he chuckled. 'He's just made me a full partner!'

'That's wonderful.'

'Care to help me celebrate? I don't suppose you're free for dinner tonight, but——'

'As it so happens, I am.' Her decision not to hibernate any longer was being put to the test, and she determined not to fail it.

He took her dancing, treating her like a single twenty-five-year-old out for a good time, rather than a serious-minded concert pianist of celebrity status, and she found herself having one of the best evenings she could remember—mindless and fun.

It was Alan himself who brought her down to earth.

'Are you still set on leaving the agency after the command performance?' he asked as he drove her home.

'You know I am. I've already told you that.'

'I was hoping you'd changed your mind.'

'I haven't.'

'Pity. We're the best in the business.'

This was too true to gainsay, so she said nothing, relieved when he took the hint and dropped the subject.

She did not repeat her evening with him, for though he was an entertaining companion, it was difficult to keep Luke out of their conversation, and she realised this would always be a barrier between them. Her aim was to forget him, and Alan would be a constant reminder.

Fortuitously, Roger's tour of duty came to an end and he was transferred from Brussels to London. Quickly he became her regular companion, making no secret of his desire to resume the intimacy they had once shared. But she wasn't ready for such a step. The memory of Luke's lovemaking—one night only, but what a night!—was still too vivid and would inhibit her response to anyone else.

Luckily this did not deter him from seeing her, no doubt in the hope that she would change her mind, and she did not rule out the possibility of eventually doing so. Meanwhile it was good to have an escort with whom she could be herself.

Peter and Gillian flew in to London the day before the royal show, eager not to miss it. Both of them looked happy, and Gillian, particularly, was glowing, the reason being disclosed the moment she came into Andrea's bedroom later that day for a chat.

'I'm pregnant,' she announced. 'I saw my doctor just before I left and he confirmed it. I'm over the moon, Annie. I feel in my bones that this time everything's going to be fine.'

'I'm sure you're right. What say we go out tonight and celebrate? I'm seeing Roger, so we can make it a foursome. I'd like you to meet him anyway. He's attending a conference in Washington tomorrow, so he won't be at the concert.'

'You've known him a long while, haven't you?'

'Yes.' Anticipating the next question, Andrea forestalled it by darting into her walk-in cupboard and emerging with a long-sleeved black lace dress. 'What do you think of this? I bought it for tomorrow night.'

'It's sensational,' Gillian enthused. 'But Luke doesn't like you wearing black on stage.'

'I couldn't care less,' Andrea shrugged. 'My contract with him ends after tomorrow's concert, so his opinion is of no consequence.'

'But he'll be there?'

'Naturally. He won't miss out on being photographed with the Queen. It's good publicity for his agency.'

Gillian ran her tongue over her lips, a gesture she always did when she had to say something she didn't like. 'Those—those things I told you about him—about his being in love with me and still wanting to marry me—they weren't true either. I said it because I *wanted* to believe it.'

At least in this respect Luke hadn't lied, Andrea thought, and said gently, 'I know.'

'That's not all I lied about,' the apology continued. 'You might as well know the worst.'

'You don't need to tell me. What's past is past.'

'That isn't true in this case.' Gillian perched on the bed and plucked nervously at the duvet. 'Remember I told you I started seeing Peter because Luke was unfaithful to me? Well, he wasn't—I made it up so I'd have an excuse for seeing Peter on the sly. *I* was the unfaithful one, not Luke.'

Andrea felt as if she had been hit in the stomach. So much of her behaviour to him had been coloured by her belief that he had played around with other women while being engaged to Gillian, and to discover it wasn't true... Recollecting how bitterly she had berated him for it, she couldn't figure out why he had allowed her to believe the worst of him. Yet would she have believed him if he *had* denied it? Knowing she wouldn't, she was overwhelmed by guilt.

'Say you forgive me?' Gillian pleaded. 'I'll do anything to put things right between you. I'll go see him and——'

'No, you won't. There's nothing to put right.'

'Of course there is. That night in Rome when I came into your dressing-room after your concert, you were full of your love for each other. And don't say you were making it up so I'd go back to Peter, because I won't wear it. You did love him, and it was a mystery to me why he returned to London and sent Alan to take his place.'

'We realised our feelings had been coloured by the excitement of the tour and——'

'Rubbish!'

'True,' Andrea insisted. 'And if you want proof, he's already smitten with Amalia Nichols. He became her manager the same time he became mine.'

'If he's managing her, he *has* to see her. It doesn't mean he loves her. If you and Luke talked things over——'

'It's already over, Gilly, so drop it. Now tell me where you fancy going tonight?'

'Anywhere so long as the food is great and we can dance!'

'Sounds like the Blue Rose. It's a new place Roger took me to last week. I'll call him and see if he can get a table.'

Nine o'clock that evening found them entering the satin-draped room that was fast becoming one of the capital's popular night spots. Andrea wore a dress she had recently bought from Hilary: vivid scarlet, the neckline high at the front and dipping almost to her waist at the back, while the tightly draped skirt made her appear slender as a reed. It was a theatrical, blatantly sexual dress, and in normal circumstances she wouldn't have bought it. But she had gone to the couturier's the day after reading about Luke and the blonde violinist, and jealousy had motivated her decision.

'We're with the two most beautiful women in London,' Roger murmured to Peter as they were shown to one of the best tables in the room, and as if to echo his comment, heads turned to watch their progress.

He ordered champagne—'How else to toast the next generation?' he teased—and they duly did so before settling down to the enjoyable task of choosing their meal.

Their first course over, Roger asked Gillian to dance, leaving Andrea to have a quiet talk with Peter.

'How are things between the two of you?' she asked.

'Better than they've ever been. Gillian can talk about the past with no regrets whatever, and that's given me much more confidence. Her falling pregnant so quickly has been an added bonus.'

He was expounding on his business and how it was growing when she glanced beyond him and saw Luke enter the room. Her heart seemed to leap into her throat and she swallowed hard, trying to hide her agitation. He was more formally dressed than usual in a charcoal-grey suit and silver-grey silk shirt that made him appear taller and thinner than she remembered. He was with three other people but the only one she noticed was the petite blonde at his side. Amalia Nichols. In the flesh she was even lovelier than her pictures: her hair a richer blonde, her skin creamy, her demeanour graceful. Jealousy, swift and sudden, pierced her, and she desperately hoped he would be shown to a table on the far side and not see her.

It wasn't to be, for a waiter led him directly past her table, making it impossible for him to ignore her.

'Good to see you,' he smiled, stepping closer to her so that the rest of his party could move past him. 'Keeping well?'

'Great. It's marvellous to take things easy after the tour.' Andrea marvelled that she sounded so calm and controlled.

'Not too easy,' he chided. 'Don't forget the Queen!'

Though he addressed the words to her, she saw he was eyeing Peter, obviously curious to know who he was. So *let* him be curious!

'Don't let me keep you from your friends,' she murmured.

'You're not.' The glint in his eyes and the mocking curve to the wide, mobile mouth showed he was all too aware that she wanted to be rid of him. Instead, he deliberately looked from her to Peter, and when it became clear she had no intention of introducing him, he smiled again and moved away.

'So I've finally seen Luke Kane in the flesh,' Peter commented.

'I didn't introduce you because I thought it might be embarrassing,' Andrea said quickly, and if Peter didn't believe her, he was too diplomatic to comment.

'Care to chance yourself to my dancing?' he suggested. 'I'm not in Roger's class, though.'

'What modesty!'

Rising, she preceded him on to the floor, talking animatedly in case Luke was looking their way. But as they danced past his table she saw that his dark head was lowered intimately towards Amalia Nichols' blonde one, and that his arm was resting on the back of her chair, almost as if he were protecting her. Luke was running true to form, she thought cynically. Same gestures but with different women!

She was glad when she noticed that Gillian and Roger had returned to their table, and Peter, alert to her mood, led her back to it. But though Luke was no longer in her line of vision, he was as clear to her as if he were sitting opposite. What unlucky turn of fate had brought him here this evening? If she had wanted proof that she was nowhere near forgetting him, she was being given it with a vengeance!

Their waiter appeared with the main course and she made a pretence of eating it, but Gillian was not easily fooled and, as their plates were removed, casually spoke to her.

'Luke came in a while ago. I take it you saw him?'

'Yes. He stopped by to say hello.'

'Is that all?'

'What else did you expect? After tomorrow's concert I'll be leaving his agency, so why should he waste time with me?'

Gillian went to reply, then thought better of it, but Andrea was aware of being watched by her and did her best to be the life and soul of the party, though afterwards she couldn't remember a single thing she had said.

It was a relief when Gillian pleaded tiredness and they could leave. Roger was disappointed the party was breaking up at a comparatively early hour and Andrea, feeling guilty for allowing him to believe she might eventually marry him—after seeing Luke tonight she knew it was going to be far into the future before she could think of any man in that way—invited him in for a nightcap and gently told him she intended concentrating solely on her career for the next few years.

'That's nothing new.' His brown eyes appraised her. 'You were doing the same when we first met but it didn't prevent us having an affair.'

'It will prevent me resuming it,' she said bluntly. 'I don't want any emotional involvement.'

'Then I'll wait till you do.'

Taking in his well muscled frame, she shook her head. 'I don't see you as a monk.'

'I'm not saying I'll be one! But you're the woman I want to marry and I'm prepared to wait for you.'

'I may never marry,' she warned, 'or I may fall for someone else.'

'You already have, but I'll still wait for you. I'm not blind, my darling,' he added as he saw her startled glance, and leaned towards her, his light brown hair looking blonder under the light of a nearby lamp. 'Your

love is either unrequited—which shows the man's a
fool!—or else he's married and can't get free.'

Refusing to say which—she wouldn't insult his intelligence by denying it completely—she merely shrugged
away an answer.

'Thanks,' he said, appreciating the reason for her silence, and downing his brandy, he rose, kissed her
lightly on the lips, and left.

CHAPTER EIGHTEEN

EXPECTING to have a restless night, Andrea slept like a top and awoke alert and full of nervous energy.

She had a noon appointment with Gavin and, before it, treated herself to an aromatherapy massage. There was nothing better than frankincense and rose for giving one a sense of well-being.

It was early afternoon when she returned home. Peter and Gillian were visiting friends, and she wandered into the music-room, drawn as always to the piano. Without thinking she picked out the notes of a Chopin étude, then realised it was one of Abraham's favourites, which she had often played for him. It seemed such a long time ago, and so much had happened to her since: love at its most passionate, followed by the bitterness of disillusion; acclamation as a concert artist in four of Europe's major cities and, most important, losing her fear of audiences.

'I thought I'd ordered you to relax today,' Alan admonished, quietly entering the room.

'I *am* relaxing.' Andrea turned to greet him. '"Music is the brandy of the damned."'

'Bernard Shaw,' he retorted. '*Man and Superman.*'

Her eyebrows rose. 'I didn't know you were a fan.'

'Of you or him?' he teased. 'Not that it matters; the answer's yes to both!'

'I can see you graduated from the same school of flattery as Luke!'

'Untrue. It comes naturally to both of us! Which reminds me—we're giving a small party for you at Inn on the Park after the concert. It's the agency's way of saying thank you to a wonderful client.'

'Oh, no! That wasn't necessary.'

'It was Luke's idea.'

Andrea nodded mutely. Luke was bound to be there, more than likely with Amalia Nichols, and seeing them together was something she could well do without.

'I'm going to the Festival Hall now to check that everything's OK.' Alan cut across her thoughts. 'A limousine will be collecting you and your family at six.'

'Yes, sir.' She saluted him. 'You're a master of efficiency.'

'I've had the best teacher,' he replied seriously. 'Luke *is*, you know.'

'Yes, I do.'

Promptly at six, Gillian and Peter and Mrs Prentice followed her into the maroon Rolls-Royce. Her housekeeper had been delighted when Andrea had given her a ticket, protesting that she hadn't expected one.

'You deserve to go more than anyone else,' Andrea had assured her. 'You put up with my moods and constant practising, so the least I can do is to let you see the end result!'

As the car crossed the Thames and approached the concert hall, some of Andrea's old nervousness returned. The building seemed massive, viewed from the bridge, and sight of the crowds already gathering outside unnerved her further. But the moment she was alone in her dressing-room she was calm again, eyeing the flowers and opening the greeting cards with pleasure untinged by fear.

Roger had sent her a magnum of champagne and his apologies for missing such a momentous occasion in her life, but she settled for a cup of black coffee and was sipping it when Alan came in.

'Anything I can get you?' he asked.

'A net to catch the butterflies in my stomach!'

'They'll disappear the instant you walk on stage.'

But they were still with her as she waited in the wings. The atmosphere in the auditorium was electric as a hushed audience sat waiting for the arrival of the Royal Family. Andrea took long, deep breaths and prayed for composure. There was a step behind her and she turned. Expecting Alan, she stifled a gasp as she saw Luke's tall, lean figure inches from hers. Her amethyst satin wrap slipped from her shoulders and slithered to the ground.

Lithely he bent to retrieve it, then lifted his eyes to study her as she stood before him, ethereal in gossamer-scalloped black lace through which her skin gleamed with the radiance of a pearl.

'I see you were determined to make me change my mind,' he murmured.

'About what?'

'Not wanting you to wear black on the platform. But you look sensational!'

Aware that flattery was his way of bolstering her confidence, she shrugged aside the compliment.

'I mean it, Andrea.'

'Then thank you.' She forced herself to meet his gaze. 'And thank you for giving a party for me tonight. It wasn't necessary, you know.'

'We always do it for special artists.'

'I thought you wanted all your artists to think they're special!'

His eyes gleamed appreciation of her come-back. 'To misquote George Orwell, some artists are more special than others!'

Before she could reply, Alan joined them. 'The royals will be here in six minutes, Luke.'

'I'd better get to the front of the house.' Abruptly he caught one of Andrea's hands and drew it to his mouth. 'Relax, my dear. You'll be magnificent.'

Andrea did not watch him go, afraid that if she did she wouldn't be able to hold back her tears.

'*You'll* be meeting the royals after the concert,' Alan said. 'It's no novelty to Luke, though. He's a great favourite with them.'

'Really?' She was surprised.

'It began professionally. Whenever they wanted to see a particular artist, they'd ask him to arrange it. Now he's more of a friend, though he never talks about it.'

Andrea couldn't help a wry smile. Had Luke experienced every pleasure? Was there nothing left to tempt him? Was he even bored with love? Hurriedly she forced her thoughts away from him, knowing it would be disastrous for her performance to stand around brooding like a lovesick schoolgirl! She flexed her fingers, then swiftly removed the diamond bracelet from around her wrist and handed it to Alan.

'Keep it for me, will you? It might distract me while I'm playing.'

A moment later she heard the National Anthem, then a momentary rustle and flurry as the audience settled back into their seats. Slowly the sounds died away and the hall fell silent. It was a tangible silence; one that

Andrea felt she could put out her hand and touch, one she had only recently learned to recognise and love.

With trembling fingers she smoothed the tiered skirt of her dress and stepped forward on to the platform. A wave of applause washed over her as she sat down before the piano, and as it died away the conductor raised his baton. From then on, she was conscious only of the music; each note a part of her soul.

Her hands crashed down on the final chord, and there was a moment of total silence before the auditorium erupted with applause. It resounded to the roof and crashed off the walls as this most reserved of British audiences clapped and cheered and stamped their feet like Italians!

Alan was waiting for her as she came off stage and led her to the reception-room behind the royal box, where she stood in line with the conductor, the leader of the orchestra, and many other of the night's participants. After a short wait the Queen walked in, and Luke, who was accompanying her, effected the introductions. Andrea gave a deep curtsy, and was thrilled when Her Majesty said how much she had enjoyed the performance.

'I've no idea what I answered,' she told Alan afterwards, though she knew exactly what Luke had murmured to her before he moved off with the Queen. 'A fine performance, Andrea. Congratulations.' The sort of thing he might have said as adjudicator at a school play; certainly not what she had expected from him. But then he had never given her what she'd expected.

'I'm sure whatever you said to the Queen was fine,' Alan assured her as he led her down the stairs to the foyer, where she espied Gillian and Peter and Mrs Prentice among the crush. The two women hugged her, joyously tearful, and Andrea, who was hanging on to her self-control by a thread, turned thankfully into Peter's strong, calm grasp.

'Welcome back to our world, Annie. For a couple of hours your music took you to the stars.'

'What a poetical thing to say!' She hugged him hard and kissed him, and as she drew away she saw Luke approaching from behind him. His face was so pale that his hair was startlingly black against it, his features taut and strained.

'See you at the party,' was all he said as he moved away to greet the music critic of a well known Sunday paper.

Andrea was disgusted that he could behave so off-handedly on the most exciting night of her life. However little he felt for her, surely he could have managed more than a few perfunctory words of congratulations? The temptation not to go to the party was great, and had it not been for disappointing Gillian and Peter, she would have pleaded illness and gone home.

Instead she went with them to the hotel, and brought an upward curve to her mouth and a tilt to her night-dark hair as she played guest of honour. Why had Luke arranged it? Was it to show the world he had no hard feelings towards her because she was leaving his agency? She could think of no other reason.

Every British music critic of note had been invited, as well as the usual celebrities guaranteed to make the news, and she felt as if she were in a replay of the party he had given for her in Rome. Except that this time Alan was beside her, while Luke stood straight and tall beside Amalia as he introduced her to people who could ease her path to success.

After an hour of continual smiling and saying the right thing, Andrea had a rip-roaring headache and knew that if she didn't lie down she would fall down.

'I don't think I can stay any longer,' she whispered to Alan. 'Would it be dreadful of me to disappear?'

'Not now.' He took in her pale face. 'Just ease out without saying goodnight and wait for me in the lobby. I'll join you as soon as I can and take you home.'

'There's no need. I'll get a cab. Please,' she added as he went to protest. 'It'll be more noticeable if we both disappear. Just tell Gillian not to rush back. I'll be fine on my own. In fact I'd prefer it.'

'Will do.' Squeezing her hand, he turned his back on her, shielding her from sight as she slipped through the door.

Not until she let herself into the calm elegance of her home did the two hammers banging in her head cease vibrating, and she collapsed into an easy chair and closed her eyes. No longer was she a confident, fêted celebrity, but a lonely woman filled with uncertainties. Indeed the only certainty was her music, and right now she would willingly have relinquished her talent and fame in exchange for the love of the right man.

How handsome Luke had looked tonight. For the first time since she had known him he had worn conventional evening clothes, no doubt in deference to the Queen. They had made him appear older, more sober, less the dazzlingly youthful impresario, more the sober businessman.

'Stop thinking of Luke!' she ordered herself, speaking aloud to give the words weight. 'He's gone from your life and you have to face it.'

As her voice died away she heard the chimes of the front doorbell. Startled, she ran into the hall, wondering who was calling so late at night. Tiptoeing to the door, she peered through the peephole. Luke! What was he doing here?

Hurriedly she unlocked the bolt and opened the door. The mellow light of the lamps behind her shone full on him as he stood there, hands at his side, face expressionless. For long seconds they stared at one another.

'You forgot to take your bracelet,' he said finally. 'Alan gave it to me.'

He made no effort to hand it to her and, politeness coming to the fore, she opened the door wider and stepped back. Silently he followed her into the drawing-room; and though his expression was still inscrutable, she was aware of a suppressed excitement in him. Or was it anger? Did he perhaps think she had deliberately forgotten her bracelet in the hope that he would bring it back to her? She was horrified by the thought.

'Alan could have returned the bracelet tomorrow,' she remarked as she perched on the edge of a chair. ' wasn't scared he'd run off with it!'

'I used it as an excuse to come here,' Luke stated, and jumping to his feet, angrily paced the floor. 'Why didn' you tell me?' he burst out. 'How the hell was I to know it was Peter...? If you knew what I suffered...'

Her bewilderment increased. 'I might if I knew what you were going on about.'

'You and Peter. I've been insane with jealousy.'

'You were jealous of my brother-in-law?'

'It wasn't until tonight—at the party—that I discovered who he was.' Luke raked a hand through his hair, ruffling its smoothness. 'When I saw you at two in the morning coming out of his room in the hotel in Rome, I couldn't believe my eyes. I recognised him instantly as the man I'd seen you with in that St John's Wood res taurant. The one you'd told me was married to a friend of yours.'

'And you thought I'd been lying—that he was really my lover?' she asked incredulously.

'What else was I to think? I assumed he'd followed you to Rome and you were meeting him secretly. Dammit, I heard you telling him that if he followed you to the Ritz in Paris he had to keep out of sight!'

'Because I didn't want Gillian to know he was there until I'd had a chance of preparing her for it.'

'I realise that now. Peter told me the whole story. But at the time...' Luke's voice trailed away and he sank on to the sofa and buried his head in his hands. 'I was burning with rage and frozen with anger. When I'd finally found the one woman with whom I wanted to spend the rest of my life, she turned out to be a two-timing, lying... God!' He groaned. 'Beats me that I managed to face you the next day. I wanted to love you and murder you; to throw you out of my life and put you in a dungeon where no one could touch you except me! I was out of my mind and I couldn't do a thing about it!'

'Except hurt me as much as you were hurting,' Andrea said shakily. 'If only you'd told me you'd seen Peter.' A thought struck her. 'How did you see me coming out of his room anyway? I thought you went back to the contessa's home?'

'I made an excuse and left as soon as I could. I'd hoped you weren't too tired to see me.'

'For an eager lover, you were very quick to think the worst of me,' she said bitterly.

'I paid for it.' He raised his head, and the bleakness in his dark eyes told her that his private hell had equalled hers. 'It wasn't until Gillian introduced me to

Peter at the party that I realised I'd made a terrible mistake.'

'You haven't exactly been pining for me since you left Rome.'

'You mean Amalia? You shouldn't believe what you read.'

'I saw the way you acted towards her.'

'With great propriety.' His voice was steady. 'You've spoiled me for other women. Oh, I tried,' he admitted with a mirthless laugh, 'if only to prove to myself I'd got over you. But it was no use. I was impotent!'

She was delighted but didn't show it. 'Is that why you're here tonight? To effect an instant cure?'

'A lifetime's cure,' he corrected. 'Don't play verbal games with me. I'm in no mood for it. I love you, Andrea, and want you to be my wife. If you're still afraid of trusting me, I'll wait for as long as it takes. But not too long. I'd like to be young enough to play football and cricket with my son, and dance at my daughter's wedding with her beautiful mother.'

'Oh, Luke!' With a tearful cry Andrea flung herself into his arms, toppling them both deep into the sofa.

Only when close to him did she appreciate the effort he had made to keep calm, for his heart was racing so fast that she couldn't count the beats.

'What a fool I was to walk out on you without telling you why,' he muttered against her lips. 'Can you forgive me?'

'If you can forgive *me* for thinking you behaved badly to Gillian, when I now know it was the other way round. She led me to believe you were a womaniser and But let's forget the past. It's over and I love you and trust you.' Emotion made it difficult for her to go on, and she buried her head into the side of his neck. Here too a pulse was hammering and she pressed her mouth to it, feeling a tremor run through him at her touch.

Lifting her arms, she held his head between her hands, losing her fingers in the richness of his thick, springy hair. She pulled his face down until their mouths met, groaning with pleasure as she felt the warm pressure of his. Expecting passion, she was surprised by his tenderness and the gentle way he caressed her: rubbing his cheek against hers, raining tiny kisses on her eyelids, the tip of her nose, the sides of her mouth, his lips finally nuzzling her ear.

'Your family won't be here for another hour at least,' he said thickly. 'Gillian gave me her word.'

Andrea's lashes fluttered. 'She never breaks it.'

'Good.' His hand caressed her breasts, his eyes glowing as the nipples stiffened against his fingers.

'Are you sure you don't want a stay-at-home wife?' she questioned tremulously.

'I want you. Home *and* away.'

'Does that mean I won't have to find a new manager?'

'Just try. From now on, your career is my second priority.'

'What's the first?'

His other hand lowered to her stomach, moving down the flatness to the gentle mound at the apex of her slender legs. Desire tremored through her and she heard the rasp of his indrawn breath as he skilfully lifted the lace skirt and slid his fingers under her silk panties, curling them into the silky hair that protected the heart of her womanhood. Desire surged through her again, and her mouth parted beneath his as her legs did the same.

With one swift movement he rose and carried her out of the room and up the stairs.

'Do you still want me to answer that question?' he asked throatily as he placed her on her bed and came down beside her.

'That won't be necessary,' she whispered, clasping him close. 'Just show me.'

**Relive the romance...
Harlequin and Silhouette
are proud to present**

by Request

A program of collections of three complete novels by the most requested authors with the most requested themes. Be sure to look for one volume each month with three complete novels by top name authors.

In June: **NINE MONTHS** Penny Jordan
Stella Cameron
Janice Kaiser

Three women pregnant and alone. But a lot can happen in nine months!

In July: **DADDY'S HOME** Kristin James
Naomi Horton
Mary Lynn Baxter

Daddy's Home... and his presence is long overdue!

In August: **FORGOTTEN PAST** Barbara Kaye
Pamela Browning
Nancy Martin

Do you dare to create a future if you've forgotten the past?

Available at your favorite retail outlet.

HARLEQUIN®   Silhouette

WHEN STOLEN MOMENTS
ARE ALL YOU HAVE . . .

The sun is hot and you've got a few minutes
to catch some rays. . . .

And what better way to spend the time than with
SUMMER MADNESS—our summer promotion that features
six new individual short contemporary stories.

SIZZLE	Jennifer Crusie
ANNIVERSARY WALTZ	Anne Marie Duquette
MAGGIE AND HER COLONEL	Merline Lovelace
PRAIRIE SUMMER	Alina Roberts
THE SUGAR CUP	Annie Sims
LOVE ME NOT	Barbara Stewart

Each story is a complete romance that's just the perfect length
for the busy woman of the nineties . . . but still providing the
perfect blend of adventure, sensuality and, of course, romance!

Look for the special displays in July and share some of the
Summer Madness!

HSM-1

 **W⊕RLDWIDE LIBRARY**